A Few Wh...

By ...

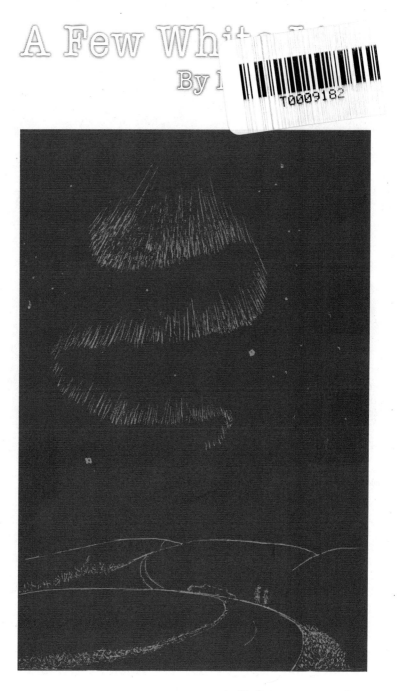

ACORNPRESS

Printed in Canada

Designed by Rudi Tusek
Edited by Terrilee Bulger

Library and Archives Canada Cataloguing in Publication

Title: A few white lies / by Lorne Elliott.
Names: Elliott, Lorne, author.
Identifiers: Canadiana 20240349261 | ISBN 9781773661216 (softcover)
Subjects: LCGFT: Novels.
Classification: LCC PS8609.L5495 F49 2024 | DDC C813/.6—dc23

Canada

Canada Council   Conseil des Arts
for the Arts   du Canada

The publisher acknowledges the support of the Government
of Canada, the Canada Council for the Arts and the Province
of Prince Edward Island for our publishing program.

ACORNPRESS

P.O. Box 22024
Charlottetown, Prince Edward Island
C1A 9J2
acornpresscanada.com

Table of Contents

Words and Music

I was staying with my dad in St. John's, with eleven days before I had to be home at Mom's, and I was standing in the front hallway when he squeezed in the door, all smiles, like he was hiding something outside.

"Look what I got for you, Thea," he said, and opened the door wide with this phony dramatic gesture. Across the street taking up two parking spaces was a purple limousine. "I won it at cards," he said.

"Great," I said, though I couldn't see what he wanted a limo for.

"Wanna go for a drive?" he said.

"I have some work to do."

"Bring it along."

I was ticked off because Grady was interrupting my writing, but I guess I was also curious, so I tucked my pencil into my notebook, dropped it into my shoulder bag and went to see what was up.

Outside a light breeze was blowing and the weather was perfect, but it was almost the first time I'd even seen the sun since I got here, and because this was Newfoundland, it would probably last about fifteen seconds.

I crossed the street as Grady ran ahead of me around the front of the limo, opened the passenger door and stood at attention like a chauffeur. "And where is it that Mademoiselle would like to go?" he said.

"Doesn't matter," I said and got inside. It was cool and roomy. Snazzy. But I was still a bit ticked off. Because of work, I guess. Once you commit, you can't let anything get in your way, and almost everything always does, like this little outing of Grady's.

He ran back around to the driver's side and got in, started the engine and pulled out onto Springdale Street, and we drove down by the overpass where the Arterial Road starts. The sun was shining but way down at the other end of the harbour a thick tongue of fog was lying in The Narrows, ready to move in. We climbed the Southside Hills and out onto the barrens, and Grady started talking in a voice like a tour bus operator.

"We have just passed the community of Shea Heights," he said. "And to the right you will see the the last surviving outhouse in Newfoundland..."

"Grady..."

"From here we will be travelling east, past (oh, what's the name of that cove?) to Cape Spear, the easternmost point of North America, where we will be closer to Ireland than to Winnipeg, which is an Ojib-Cree word meaning 'muddy water'..."

"You're losing it, Grady," I said. "A tour-bus guy would know the name of that cove, and that thing about Winnipeg is out of place."

"Passengers are requested to refrain from interrupting as we proceed on our journey to the easternmost point of North America..."

"You've already said that."

"...First passing... um... Maddox Cove."

"That's cheating. You saw the sign."

"...Home of Sydney Maddox."

"Who's he?"

"Mayor of Maddox Cove."

"So?"

"Give me a break," he said in his real voice. "Not a lot of things about Maddox Cove you *can* say."

"Actually, there is," I said. "Maddox Cove is named after a type of digging tool, a mattock, that was found there by an archeologist from Memorial University and which, because the Indigenous population did not work iron, is believed to have been left behind by Irish Monks."

"Really?"

"You're not the only one who can BS, Grady."

He glanced over at me, impressed. "Very good, Thea. Feeling better?"

"I wasn't sick."

"No. Just a bit grumpy."

◆-‖◆‖-◆

We arrived at Cape Spear, brown and weather-beaten with its big toad of a lighthouse, and we got out and stood in a steady cold wind blowing out of a clear sky. In front of us you could look right out to sea, but if you looked north you saw that bank of fog had moved right into The Narrows now, and Cabot Tower was floating on a cloud.

"So what do you think?" he said.

"About the view?"

"Yeah. Sure. And the limo."

"It's okay I guess. A bit ostentatious."

"What's that mean?"

"Showy."

"Well, I am in showbusiness, so it's totally appropriate. If I was a *poet*, now, that would really be ostentatious."

"Osten*tatious*. And what do you got against poets?"

"Awful people. Never bathe or cut their hair. And they certainly wouldn't be caught dead driving across the country with their father, for example."

I didn't know what he was talking about, and then I was distracted by what might have been a whale way out in from of us, a fist of spray. I told Grady and he looked for a bit and then said "Or maybe a gannet. When they dive sometimes the splash looks like a whale blowing."

"Too bad," I said. "I wanted to see a whale."

He nodded, then waited a while. "So what about it?" he said.

"About what?"

"Driving across country to get you home."

It's one of the things that really ticks me off about Grady. He can never just come out and say what he wants, just drops hints until you make the connections yourself, and then because it's like *you* thought of it, you end up agreeing to what he wanted to do.

"Grady!"

"What?"

"Well, what? I'm just supposed to just say "let's go!""

"Why not? It'll be great. "

"You said we'd be here for another week."

"Yes."

"And now you're saying you want to just take off?"

"Things change."

"That's Not Good Enough!"

"No need to scream, Thea."

"I'm Not Screaming. THIS IS SCREAMING!" And I've got a loud voice, so that stopped him.

"Okay, okay, okay," he said. "But Jeez Thea, I'm just asking. We could be at the ferry in Port Aux Basques by midnight. Make the last boat tonight if we leave soon."

"Why?"

"Why not? It'll be fun."

But dammit, I wasn't going to just give in to everything he said. My life would be a mess. And I'd told myself that I would finish my book of haiku by the time I left St. John's.

I got into the car and sat there and didn't say anything while he drove back to town. I took out my notebook and corrected some punctuation.

"What are you writing?"

"Haiku."

"What's that?"

"Japanese poems."

"Since when do you speak Japanese?"

"Since never. It's a Japanese *form* of poetry."

"Read me some."

"You can buy a copy when it's published."

"Come on, Thea. Is it about me?"

"Why would it be about you?"

"It *is* about me, isn't it?"

"You're not the centre of the universe, Grady."

"I am to me."

"Well, that's kind of sad."

Grady puffed out his cheeks, breathed out, then said like he was reciting:

"Oh Father dear, I write to you,
A poem because if I
Ever seem grumpy,
Mean or chumpy
Please forgive me my

Moods all pouty,
Snarky, louty,
And forgive me too
For my snotty attitude,
Cuz Father, I love you."

Then he gave me this big grin, the show-off.

He can do that sort of stuff, make up poems on the spot, and I got to admit, it got me interested.

"Did you just think that up?"

"Yep."

"How?"

"I'm a genius."

"No. Really."

"We're never appreciated while we're alive."

"Seriously Grady. How do you make up poems just like that?"

"Jeez, Thea. I been writing songs all my life."

"Yeah, but they're, like, country songs."

"And country songs are what? *Beneath* you?"

"They're beneath everybody."

"Yeah? Well I'm sure if you went to Japan you'd hear somebody say that those hokies of theirs are stupid and country music is the height of art."

But I'd ticked him off, so I guess I could cheer up now. (Jesus, *people*, I thought)

"They are called 'haiku', Grady. And if you think they're so stupid, then you've never tried writing one."

Grady's temper only lasts about five seconds anyway, unlike Mom who can hold a grudge for, like, decades.

"What are the rules?" he said.

"Five syllables on the first line, seven on the second, then five again for the last."

"Where are the rhymes?"

"They don't rhyme."

"Easy-peasy. That's what it sounds like if you ask me. Easy-peasy."

"Yeah, well, just try it."

"Five, seven, then five? That's what you say's a haiku? Five, seven, then five?"

"Yes. Go ahead. Try it."

"I just did."

"Did what?"

Grady took one hand off the steering wheel and counted the syllables.

"Five, seven, then five?
That's what you say's a haiku?
Five, seven, then five?"

"Yeah but..."

"Easy-Peasy, that's what it sounds like if you ask me. Easy-peasy."

It ticked me off, to tell the truth. It was easy for him. And I didn't want to ask, but I had to. "How'd you do that?"

"Don't count the syllables, Thea. Just get the rhythm in your head. Dum da dum dum dum. That's five. Listen to the sound. There's another one right there. "List-en to the sound." Get it? Now. Dum da dum dum, dum dum dum, that's seven. Hell, Thea, it should be dead simple for you. Remember those skipping songs you used to do?

"What are you talking about?"

"Had a little car, Nineteen forty eight
Went around the corner
Slammed on the brakes
Brakes didn't work, went to jail
How many bottles of ginger ale?"

"You been lurking around schoolyards lately, Grady?"

He smiled. "Used to hear you singing that back home. I'd be inside, making some demo tapes or something and you'd be outside with whosit, you're friend?"

"Marcia."

"Yeah, Marcia. Once I even held the microphone up to the window and taped you, then patched it into that CD I was making. Just as the last song fades out we hear you in the background."

"Do I get any royalties?"

"I lost money on that record."

"Big surprise. Anyhow, what's that gotta do with writing poetry?"

"You weren't overthinking them."

"I didn't write them."

"No, but it's the same idea. You learned the rhythm without even knowing, so they came out natural. Just like country music."

"I see what you're saying," I said. "How about this, then?

> Dumb Dumb Dumb Dumb Dumb
> That's what country music is
> Dumb Dumb Dumb Dumb Dumb."

"Not bad," said Grady. "Except you're wrong."

—◦┼┼◦◦┼┼◦—

We got back to the house, and Grady couldn't find a place to park so he let me off and drove around the block looking for a spot big enough for the limo, which was going to be a problem with that car, I could see. I went to the front door, but I didn't have the key with me, so I swore and blamed Grady for a bit and then sat on the front steps and counted my breaths till I calmed down.

It was still nice weather. Warm in the sun but with that fog in the East End keeping the air cool underneath. Right now that same fog would be rolling up Cochrane Street into Bannerman Park and when it moved over you it was like being magically transported into another season.

I liked St. John's. I liked walking to the University library where the nice lady helped me get whatever I wanted from the stacks, and on weekends I liked hiking around Signal Hill. But now apparently we'd be leaving, although I could always throw a fit and Grady'd probably give up on the idea.

On the other hand the idea of taking off like that kind of appealed to me. A girl once asked Bertrand Russell how to become a writer and he told her to write as much as possible and get as much experience in life as she could. And I'd never driven across country, and there was no way you could cross more of this country than from Newfoundland to Haida Gwaii. It was just about as far as you could go and still be in Canada. I used to think that was the reason my parents lived where they did, to be as far away from each other as possible.

The limo was comfortable, too, I'll say that. And if I got bored I could always read.

On the road with Dad...Wants to go out west, he says...Road just rolls along, he says.

And it was in fact easier to write haiku when you didn't count. (Though that last haiku sounded like one of Grady's country songs, for godsakes.)

I watched a cat press his back against the inside of a window on the other side of the street, doing her cat-stretch extra-luxuriously, trying to make me jealous that she was nice and warm inside while I was out on the street.

Then Grady came around the corner below, and when he saw me he danced up the street like in some garbage Hollywood musical. When he got to me it took him a while to get his breath back. He's not as young as he sometimes likes to pretend.

"So what do you think, Thea?" he said.

"I think we should get inside."

"I mean about leaving."

"How are we gonna eat?"

"Buy food on the way. We can bring some food from here, too."

"Do you have enough money for gas?"

"Sure. And if we run low we can pick up hitchhikers and ask them to chip in."

"Where do we sleep?"

"In the limo. I can take the front seat."

"You snore."

"I've never heard it."

"That's because when you *do* snore, you're asleep, you dough-head."

"Well, I can pitch a tent, then. And like I say, you can have the back all to yourself. It's a great ride. The only problem is there's no radio. Somebody ripped it off."

"Good."

"Why?"

"Well, Grady, the music you listen to is, like, pathetic."

"Yeah? Well, who do you listen to?"

And he'd caught me off-guard, because I didn't actually listen to a lot of music. My friend Marcia, though, was a big fan of somebody who she had posters of on her bedroom wall and everything. "Daisy Ratzinger," I said.

"Really?" said Grady.

"What? You don't approve I suppose?" Because Daisy Ratzinger's a protest singer, and Grady isn't exactly on the forefront of positive political change.

"Not that," he says. "It's just, I used to work with her."

I looked over to see if he was kidding. "You?"

"Yep."

"*The* Daisy Ratzinger."

"The only one I know."

I couldn't believe it. Marcia would have a fit. "When?"

"A few years ago." He didn't even seem to think it was that important.

"Why would..?" I said, then stopped.

He raised his eyebrows. "Why would somebody as talented and glamorous as the Great Daisy Ratzinger stoop to work with such a lonely pathetic figure as your father? Is that what you're trying to say?"

"Well... yeah."

"Thanks."

"So, why?"

"We had the same management for a while, and she wasn't as big as she is now."

"So, like, you were in her band?"

"I was her warm-up act."

"Well... You must be, like, rich."

"Hah!"

"Why not?"

"That's not the way it works. That last tour of hers I would've done better just booking my own show in bars."

"The Rat Singer's Lounge Tour?"

"That's the one."

"Me and Marcia were about to take the bus to Pritchet for that!"

Some kids from school actually did go see that show, and they said it was awesome... And then I remembered something that one of the kids had also said, that the warm-up act had sucked.

And for some reason, a line from William Blake came into my head: "Cherish Pity, lest you drive an angel from your door." And I looked at Grady who was gazing off down toward the harbour.

"Sure, Grady," I said. "Let's do it."

"Drive across country?"

"Yeah."

"That's great, Thea. You won't regret it!" He was smiling, now, his real smile, not his jokey showbiz one.

We got our stuff together and Grady cleaned out the fridge and put it all in a pillow case. I walked down to Pico's Groceteria and Confectionary and picked up some sugar and tea and bread and cheeze, and there are never any shopping carts in these little corner stores, so my hands were getting full when I got to the shelf that had the sugar and I put the box of sugar cubes in my bag to carry to the cash, and then I started thinking about how Grady was once again getting what he wanted like he always does, and I started to get ticked off about being manipulated and not finishing my book of haiku before I left St. John's like I told myself I would, so I concentrated on my breathing again as I waited for the old woman in front of me to buy a lotto ticket and have a good long chin-wag about the weather, and then I finally got to pay for the food, and I was outside and halfway back up Springdale Street when I remembered I hadn't paid for the sugar, which was still in my bag.

I had shop-lifted, even though it was by mistake. But I was not going to go back down the hill again to return it, and it was only like three bucks, so I thought to hell with it. And to tell the truth, it felt kinda cool. I was on the road, now, a drifter who made her own rules.

When I got to the house Grady was packing his possessions, which were pathetic, basically his guitar and some socks, and I went upstairs and got my clothes and sleeping bag and books, brought them down and arranged my books in the back of the limo. They fit perfectly into the drinks cabinet, and looked like one of those old time libraries in a mansion all lined in wood. We got everything ready and double-checked, and Grady locked up and left a note for the guy he was borrowing the house from.

Then we got in the limo and Grady pulled out and drove down the hill and onto Arterial Road, and we were on our way to Haida Gwaii, ive thousand six hundred and thirty-three kilometers away, with eleven days to do it in.

2

The Big To-do

The reason I'd come to Newfoundland to live for a while with Grady was after this big to-do at school in Prince Rupert, which is which is where I usually live with Mom, when we are not out on Haida Gwaii for the summer, taking care of the Café.

At first they said I couldn't quit school, at least not without my parents' consent, but then the principal, Reggie Barnes, talked to Mom and she told him that I could do anything I bloody well wanted, which was the first I'd ever heard of it, though she probably only said that because Mom hates Reggie's guts. Then the Department of Education got involved and said I would be denied an education, though I was thinking *what* education? I mean, I've always done good on exams, particularly geography, which I even won a prize for in grade eight, a big atlas, which was kind of pointless. I mean, thanks and everything, but I already know everything in that book or I wouldn't have won it in the first place. And what they never figured out was that the reason I was into Geography so much was that from about the age of thirteen I've wanted to run away from home.

This was all just after the time I was making this lame attempt to act like a "normal" human being, whatever that is. I even signed up for the student entertainment committee, partly because Grady's in showbusiness, and also because my friend Marcia had already signed on.

But it was kind of pointless. We'd sit around trying to think up a theme for the costume dance, for instance, and first somebody suggested 'the sixties,' but we'd done that the year before. So, somebody else said how about a sci-fi theme, but that meant a lot of tinfoil and glue and a big environmental footprint apparently, so then some-body suggested "beatniks," which everybody said okay to, and I said okay to as well, just to go along with every-body else, though I didn't have a clue what a "beatnik" even looked like.

So I went to the library and found some photos and mainly they looked like a bunch of scruffy students standing around smoking cigarettes, which, for people who were supposed to be so intellectual is a pretty stupid habit.

Anyhow, I went down to the Salvation Army and found a black turtleneck and some black jeans and when I tried them on, I mean, I'm not vain or anything, but I gotta say, I did look pretty cool. So I kept dressing like that, and that's when I started reading Bertrand Russell, because he wrote the kind of books that somebody who dressed like me would probably read.

Apparently the beatniks were all into philosophy, see, so I went to the library again and looked for something I could carry around as a sort of prop, and in the philosophy section was Bertrand Russell's *Autobiography*, and I started carrying it around in my shoulder bag or taking it out to read when people started bothering me.

The point is that at first I was just being a poser, I know that, using the book as a sort of fashion accessory for godsakes. But when I did actually dip into it, I found, surprise surprise, that it was, like, *good*. All about him being born into the English aristocracy, his grandfather the Prime Minister, and growing up in a big mansion with a brother who was a bit of a hell-raiser but who turns him onto mathematics, which he says was the only thing in his adolescence that kept him from committing suicide.

And just that alone, having somebody pointing out that sometimes being a teenager isn't all that excellent, well, it was honest, anyway, and you knew now at least that there was somebody else somewhere who had thought something like that, even way back then. It was all really clear writing, too, and you got the impression that he didn't care what other people thought about him. And I started to think that maybe I'm not that weird after all, or maybe, what's more likely, everybody's weird, it's just nobody mentions it because we're all trying to fit in.

So that was the end of my last lame attempt at joining things, and I owe it all to Bertrand Russell. He's cool. And if he were teaching you, he'd be trying to make sense of things and keep pushing the subject along to where it starts to fall apart, because that's where it gets interesting.

He wouldn't be like our Algebra teacher, Barclay Perth, that's for sure, who wants everybody to think he's so incredibly intellectual by acting snide and putting himself above everybody else. He even talks with this English accent for godsakes, though I know for a fact that he's from, like, Vernon.

The day I quit school he was teaching us about sets and subsets. He draws this circle on the blackboard with a smaller circle inside it, just so, like an extra-neat drawing would make it more understandable for us doughheads who he's been sentenced to teach. Then he says, "Any definable collection is called a set. And if we let P be the set of all fruit...." And he points at the outside circle. "...and Q be the set of apples..." and he writes the letter Q inside the small circle, "...then Q is included in P."

Great. So what he's saying is that an apple is a fruit? Because most of us are way ahead of him on that vital bit of info.

I'm sick of it all, and have been for about a week, but today I'm just sitting there with my text book not even open.

"Thea? What's going on?" he asks me finally.

So I say, "What's the point?"

"Oh? Like the universe is running out, like, man? Is that it?"

And I know I say "like" a lot, but I don't say "man," so he's just clumping me into some convenient category, and I thought I might point out that maybe he's taking these sets and subsets a bit too seriously, but instead I just say, "No. It's just that this particular stupid subject doesn't have any meaning."

"Just because you're wearing black, Thea, doesn't mean you're deep," he says, and the rest of the class laughs, and it ticks me off.

"Well, look at you," I say. "I mean, tweed with leather patches? Jeez, Barclay, where's the pipe?"

"No need to get personal, Thea," which was kind of rich since he started it, and then he adds, "Now, tell me why you think it's meaningless."

"You tell *me* what it means."

"You can't prove anything unless you first break it down into different categories."

"What if categories have no meaning?"

"But they do."

"Well, I disagree."

"Then prove it!" he says like he'd cornered me into joining the lesson with his peerless teaching technique.

But I wasn't just mouthing off. "Russell's Paradox," I said.

"Sorry?"

"If you consider the set of all things that are not members of themselves, then if that set *is* a member of itself, it's *not* a member of itself, and if it isn't a member of itself, then it is."

Don't even try to get your head around it the first time. I had to reread it for about a week, and find examples of what it was talking about, and finally I'd get a glimmer of what it was saying, and then it was gone.

And that's because it's not real, just a construction of words and logic.

But it felt good, reeling it off like that to Barclay, so I looked right at him and added in a bratty voice, "...Man."

And he stared back at me, furious.

And that's when I knew, see, even though I had a point, he wasn't interested in the truth. He just wanted to be considered the smartest guy in the room.

So I stood up, picked up my books, and walked out of the class and out of the school and I kept walking till I got back home.

"Thea?" said Mom, and she looked at the clock on the wall. "What happened?"

"I quit," I said.

"But..."

"They're teaching things that have been disproved since forever."

Mom tried to convince me to give it another try but I said no way, so next day I just lay in bed reading William Blake and probably getting a better education. Blake himself never even went to school, and now they're teaching him there, so that should tell you something.

The next day after that, though, Mom took me to the Doctor.

Mom tells him what's happened and he asks Mom if I have exhibited any other strange behaviour, so of course Mom has to tell him about how I cut my hair, which was like a year ago and was a mistake, I'll admit, but it was for the beatnik dance and I was just trying to, like, get into *character*, for godsakes. So the night before the dance, I went after my hair with some scissors, glanced in the mirror and thought, that's pretty exotic, then went downstairs to see Mom. She looked at me and she just *screamed.* And if you if think I got a loud voice, when Mom's full throttle, honest-to-God, she could fell trees.

She leaps into action and phones in an emergency hairdressing appointment at Emma's Salon de Coiffure, then grabs me by the arm and drags me out and bundles me to the car like she's keeping me hidden from any paparazzi who might want to blackmail us, and she spins out of the driveway, and it's only two blocks to Emma's but she manages to run three lights and a stop sign, then screeches to a halt in Emma's driveway and bundles me out of the car and into the Salon, and Emma looks and gasps and says 'Oh-my-God-in-heaven-above'. And she sits me down, and the whole time Mom is telling, in horrifying detail, the harrowing tale of how just fifteen minutes before I'd come downstairs, and she starts sobbing, and I say, "Shave it all off. I don't care."

And they think about it and consult each other, saying that they could always tell people that I was in chemotherapy.

Anyhow, Emma does something with it, and if you ask me the result is pretty boring, but nobody does ask me, they never do, and either you care what you look like or you don't, so I thought, let them do what they want with it.

So she does and Mom thanks her and then bursts into tears, and they go have tea.

And I say, "What's the problem? It'll grow back."

"Yeah, in six months," says Mom, and I think, so what?

But then it's like I see how it's easy for me, because I'm going to be around for years, but she's like forty-five or something and so is really quite old and is going to die a lot sooner.

It was like a vision, the kind that I've always had, and maybe everybody has, but which I didn't recognize for what they were until I started reading William Blake.

The first poem of his I ever read was printed up in Volume Two of Russell's *Autobiography*, and the first time *Russell* heard one was on a staircase in his college where some other student recited "The Tyger" and Russell almost fainted when he heard it.

So I figured I'd better check this out and took out a book of Blake's poems from the library. And at first I have to say that a lot of them sounded like meaningless gibberish, but that's because Blake was a lunatic who was transcribing his visions and not just putting down things that already have nice handy words assigned to them. I mean, Bertrand Russell lays things out real clearly, and maybe that's because he's a mathematician and he's only dealing with provable things, but Blake's a poet and he's going into that big fog out there, and sometimes he stumbles back with something that actually *means* something. And maybe Bertrand Russell put that poem in the front of his autobiography because he recognized that his own way of straight-forward logical thinking wasn't necessarily the be-all and end-all. And that's when I thought that I'd become a poet, and make Philosophers faint on staircases.

The Doctor wouldn't be interested in all that, though, and if I started to recite Blake to him, he'd probably have me lobotomized.

Then he asked Mom if I had done anything else out of the ordinary and Mom says I talked to cats. And I'm thinking "yeah, who doesn't? and incidentally, thanks for ratting me out Mom." And the Doctor looks at me and asks, "What do you say?"

"I don't know, like 'Here, kitty, kitty'."

"I see. Do they ever answer?"

"Yes."

"Really?" he posed his pencil. "How do they answer?"

"Mostly, like 'Meow'."

"So they do not answer in your language?"

"No," I said. "They answer in their language."

"Do you understand what they are saying?"

"Sure."

"Well, what are they saying?"

"Things like 'I want to be petted', or 'I want some milk'. Things like that."

"I see. Do you ever talk to plants?"

"No. But Mom does."

He looked at Mom like there was probably some more business coming his way, then back at me. "Do you ever hear voices?"

"Yes."

"Aha..." he said. "And what do they say to you?"

"One just asked me if I ever heard voices."

But he doesn't twig. "Just now?" he said.

"Yes."

He made a note. "Can you still hear them?"

"There's only one."

And now he started to get quite excited like maybe he's the first psychiatrist ever to witness a patient undergoing auditory hallucinations or something. "And you hear this voice now?"

"Yes."

"What's it saying?"

"It's asking me what it's saying."

"What who's saying?"

"The voice."

"The voice is asking you what the voice is saying?"

"Yeah. Kind of pointless, eh?"

But he still didn't get it. He made a note, then leaned back in his chair and knit his brow and tapped his teeth with his pencil.

"Is it male or female?"

"Male."

"Ah."

"Is that significant, Doctor?" Mom said, which is something she must've heard on TV.

"Possibly," he said.

So I thought I'd put him out of his misery. "Look, you dough-head," I said. "It's *your* voice I'm hearing."

He didn't like that, being fooled, and probably being called a dough-head didn't help either. He got cold and serious and he had the same look in his eye that Barclay had. Clearly I was becoming an enemy of the state.

"What I meant," he said, "was do you ever hear voices in your head?"

"Yes."

"Auditory hallucinations?"

"How would I know if they're hallucinations or not?" He thought. "Good point."

But I *do* hear voices, sometimes. At night, for instance, just before I drop off to sleep, a voice shouts something at me and I snap awake. Marcia says she hears them too sometimes, so it's not just me. I mean, like, who doesn't? And I think if you asked everybody and they were honest, you'd find that most people do, they just don't want to admit it because they're trying to fit in and be normal, which is kind of sad.

Anyhow, the Doctor had a long talk with Mom with all sorts of gobbledeglook about integrating the family unit and re-connecting with a community identity, but basically, he didn't know what to do with me and the Board of Education didn't either. Mom said she didn't know how she was going to be able to deal with it all, that she had to go shut the Café in Haida Gwaii for the winter or the bank would take it back.

But then she got Marcia's mom got in touch with her sister, who was a nurse in St. John's, Newfoundland who looked up Grady, who apparently said sure, he'd take care of me. So Mom cashed in the frequent flyer points she'd gotten from buying supplies for the Café, and drove me to Pritchit to catch a plane to Vancouver to make the connection to Toronto that points east on a clear night, flying over a web of light below with the lights getting fewer the further north you looked. First time I'd ever flown, and it was like a vision, but it was real.

And a month later, here I was getting ready to cross back over all that country with Grady.

It was going to be an adventure, and would give me all sorts of stuff to write about. At the very least it would be exciting.

3

Exodus

"I'm bored, Grady."

"We've just started."

"There's nothing to do."

"Look at the landscape."

"I don't have to look at the landscape. I already know what the landscape looks like. Exactly the same as it did a half hour ago and a half hour before that. Like Signal Hill without the ocean."

"I thought you liked Signal Hill."

"I do. But it's got ocean. How come we can't see the ocean?"

"Road doesn't go that way."

"Why not?"

"It would take too long to get the fish to market."

"What fish?"

"True. Mostly fished out here nowadays. Get the lumber to market, then."

But the trees here were like, pathetic, at least compared to British Columbia. We passed a few scrawny
birch with their upper branches purple-brown like the
paws of a Siamese cat. I sighed, opened my notebook
and wrote.

Cut down the forests
Then take the money and move
Some place nice with trees

Which wasn't a bad haiku, if I do say so myself. And
the right number of syllables, which I didn't count as I
wrote.

I popped another sugar cube into my mouth from the
box in my handbag.

"Where'd you get those?" said Grady.

"Stole 'em."

"Really?"

"Didn't mean to."

"How can you not mean to steal something?"

So I told him, pointing out that it was only because I
was angry at him that made me forget to pay for the
sugar, so it was his fault really.

"Well, if it was a mistake, I suppose," he said. "Still,
you shouldn't steal stuff."

"Who says?"

"Um ...The ten commandments?"

Although he's my father he likes to act like he's just
some sort of older friend or advisor. And you could tell
he was uncomfortable about the conversation getting
religious. Which was interesting.

"I'll bet you can't even name the ten commandments, Grady."

"Well, can you?

"Yep," I lied. "I learned them in Sunday school."

"When did you ever go to Sunday school?"

"Two years ago, when Mom caught religion. Then the Reverend slapped the makes on her, and she became a Buddhist again."

The Reverend had never actually slapped the makes on Mom, I was just seeing whether I could make him jealous, and I don't know quite why I did that, though I did flash back on that cat in the window.

Anyhow, he didn't take the bait. "Sunday School?" he said, rolling his eyes. "Man, you try to raise them right."

"You never raised me at all," I said. Which is true. He hadn't. And for the last three years he'd disappeared entirely.

But he let that slide.

"So she's back to being a Buddhist?"

"Nope. She's a pantheist now."

"What's that mean?"

"She believes in everything."

"That sounds like your mom, alright," he said. But I guess he didn't want to start criticizing her around me. "What are you?" he said.

"Agnostic."

"Gesundheit."

"Grady..."

"Just kidding. What's that mean, though? Like an atheist?"

"No. It's not that we don't believe in God. It's just that we haven't made our minds up yet." I was speaking like a dues-paying member of some organized system, but actually I'd only read about it in Bertrand Russell.

"Doesn't sound like much of a system of belief," said Grady.

So I said something I'd picked up from one of Russell's friends. "I do not believe in belief."

"Then how can you believe that?" said Grady, which as far as I knew was an argument that neither Russell nor his friend had ever run into.

We stopped for gas by the highway in Gander, and Grady got out and filled up, talking with another customer at the pumps about the limo, how it handled, how much gas it took, boy-talk. I went inside the station and looked over the magazine racks for something to read, but their covers all showed either girls with cleavage or guys with dead animals they'd just shot, so I went to ask for the key to the bathroom and the guy at the counter said it was out of order but that I could go to the motel next door. So I went out and across a little ditch to the end room nearest the station where a maid was cleaning up, and I told her that they said I could use their bathroom, and she said yes, dear, sure, and let me go through to it as she started to haul her cleaning cart and vacuum cleaner to the next room.

When I came out of the bathroom, on the way back outside I stopped and listened for the maid who was vacuuming next door now, then took two quick steps between the beds and opened the bedside drawer and there it was, a Gideon's bible.

But standing there flipping through the pages I couldn't find where the ten commandments even were, and then the vacuum in the room next door switched off suddenly, so almost without thinking I dropped the bible into my bag and stepped to the centre of the room just as the maid came back around.

"Finished, dear?" she said.

"Yep," I said. "Thanks," and I walked past her outside and back across the parking lot and ditch to where Grady was just coming out of the station from paying for the gas.

"It's not a guzzler, not for its size," he said to me. "But it ain't exactly light on gas, either."

Bibles are free anyway, mostly, and as far as I can see, the whole point of the Gideons is to distribute them, so if you looked at it a certain way I was just helping to do their job.

But I'd never stolen anything before, except that sugar, which was a mistake so it doesn't count. My three volumes of Russell's *Autobiography* and *The Portable William Blake* were overdue by two months from the library in Prince Rupert, but I preferred to think of that as a sort of extended loan and I totally intended to return them, eventually, once I'd learned everything in them. And if they wanted to track me down and take them back, go ahead, but that would mean the library is stopping people from educating themselves, which is what a library is supposed to encourage, I thought.

When I got back into the limo that stolen bible was weighing on me, though, because it's like, a bible, and I know that's only superstition. I mean if it was a magazine I'd stolen, it should be the same as far as feeling guilty goes, or worse actually, because magazines are never given away but always sold. And then I thought that maybe that was what made what I'd done wrong, because bibles are like a different sort of book, not that I think God wrote it or anything, but people do give them away, not for money but just from one human being to another, and maybe that's what made them, I dunno, *sacred*.

I took it out of my bag and it felt heavy as lead.

Grady glanced over and did a double take.

"Is that a bible?"

"I brought it with me from home. I'm looking up the ten commandments."

"Which one?"

"Stealing."

"Number eight," he said. "Exodus 20 and somewhere in Deuteronomy."

I looked at him.

"My dad *was* a minister, Thea, and he said."

I'd forgotten. "Yeah. But you only ever talk about him like he was a mean old SOB."

"He was. And a hypocrite... Oh man, don't get me started..." Then he added in his doomsday voice, "For hark ye, The Lord thy God is a jealous God..."

And even though he was trying to be funny, it started to creep me out a little.

The country we were driving through now was kinda spooky, too, with a weird thin fog that had moved in over the highway and a wind that every now and then shook the limo. In the rear view mirror I saw a raven flap down to pick at something on the road then flap off into the grey behind us.

"For verily I say unto you," said Grady, like a mock preacher again, "The Lord thy God is a jealous God..."

"Okay, Grady. I got it."

"I can feel it in me. God is speaking through me."

"Stop it, Grady."

"For look ye, it is written..." and he pointed ahead through that thin fog.

"Where? What are you talking about?"

"Soon it shall be revealed."

"I don't know what I'm even supposed to be looking for."

"Ye shall know it when ye see it."

"Knock it off, Grady! I swear to God..."

"Swear not to God, Thea, for that which you swear on shall be visited back upon ye... There!"

And he pointed out into the fog as a billboard loomed into sight like Grady had conjured it up, its message written in big letters:

BE SURE THAT YOUR SINS WILL FIND YOU OUT-NUMBERS 32:23.

And I screamed. A real ear-splitter.

Grady shot a stare over at me and nearly swerved off the road. "Christ!"

"That... sign..."

"Calm down, Thea! It was a joke! I knew it was coming up! I've passed here hundreds of times!"

For about a quarter of a second I was, like, *speechless* with anger.

Then I saw a way to get even.

"No," I said, in a dead voice. "It was fated that I should see it."

"What?" He looked over at me again and I kept staring straight ahead into the fog.

"I see it all now. It was God's will." Because if Grady thinks he can play with *my* head, he'll have to be taught different.

"Thea, I was messing with you..." And he sounded truly worried. Good.

"No, Father. It was God's will working through you." And I kept staring ahead like I'd seen something big and terrifying.

"Look Thea..."

"I stole the bible," I said in my dead voice.

"What?"

"When you were in the gas station, I went to the motel and stole it. I confess it. And now I shall burn for eternity in Hell."

"Thea..." He was really worried now, but I kept staring straight ahead of me like a possessed child.

"Oh, what am I to do? I can't throw it away, for that would be a sin, too. And I can't burn it. No. I must carry it around with me like a mark of shame." I looked over at Grady, who was almost terrified now.

"Look, Thea. Here's a gas station coming up. We'll stop for a bit."

He pulled in and parked away from the pumps, turned off the engine, took a breath, and looked at me. "Now, Thea, I'm really *really* sorry about playing that joke on you. I thought it'd be a laugh. I had no idea you were so, I dunno, *religious*. The church here just puts those signs up, and they don't mean anything."

"It was God's Will."

"No, really, it wasn't, Thea. It's some lame preacher trying to scare the bejeezus out of his congregation. I saw my father do it hundreds of times. And, if you want, we can turn around and go right back to St. John's and you can get your flight next Tuesday. I'll get the money together somehow. And you can return that bible on the way back, and make everything right..."

There was something wrong with that, and it made me pause, and broke my rhythm.

So I said in my normal voice, "You're not the only one who can BS, Grady."

And he looked at me and stopped, and then barked out a laugh.

"Thank God!... I thought... I... I don't know *what* I thought... Ha! ...Man! You got me good!"

He was so relieved I was almost sorry I'd put him through it.

But there was that thing he'd said.

"What did you mean that 'you'll get the money some-how'?" I asked him.

His smile froze, and to cover for himself he started the car and put it into gear.

"What? When?" he said, and he pulled out onto the highway.

"Just now. You told me if I wanted we could go back to St. John's and you could get the money together somehow."

"What money?" he said. The old switcheroo.

"That's what I'm asking."

"Well, Thea...I...have no idea... I was babbling. You got me so good!"

And I could have kept asking, and looking back maybe I should have, but I had something on him now that I could bring up any time I really wanted to know.

What can I say? It was a long drive.

We got to Port Aux Basques with a good twenty minutes to spare before the ferry left and I hid in the backseat under a blanket so we didn't have to pay for an extra passenger, and we rolled into the big metal room below decks where they dragged some chains to keep the car from rolling around, and once everybody was aboard, the door of the ferry hissed and clanked shut and the boat pulled away. We went upstairs to the cafeteria and had some fries and tea, and Grady found a place to throw his sleeping bag down on the platform up beside where the banister rail bent around, and I went out onto the back deck and watched the seagulls swooping in and out of the dark beyond the lights of the boat, with the wake boiling behind.

I think I might've had a vision there. Something about Time. Or maybe it was just something I'd read which had come back to me.

But now it was cold so I shivered and went back down to the car deck and into the limo. Before I went to sleep I looked in my stolen bible for Numbers 32:23, which is the chapter and verse that the sign had said to "Be sure that my sins would find me out."

It turns out they were taking the verse totally out of context, and that all Moses had talked about in Numbers

32:23 was if you didn't cross the river and beat up on some other tribe, then God would be ticked off at you and would find you out for *that particular* sin, which was the sin of, like, *not* killing a lot of other people.

That billboard really was just trying to scare you, like Grady had said, and I didn't feel bad about having stolen the bible now.

4

Bound for Moncton

We got up next morning just as the ferry was coming into North Sydney, the whole boat shaking
and shuddering like we were in an earthquake and I
went upstairs and met with Grady in the cafeteria and
had a quick breakfast of one green banana and a coffee,
which was awful, and then this robot voice on the PA
told us that we were supposed to go down to our vehi-
cles and wait till the ferry docked. Before I went,
though, I took one brochure from every slot on a big
wall of tourist info.

"Did you pick up anything about Moncton?" said
Grady. "Moncton's a real interesting town."

Which seemed like a very un-Grady-like thing to
say and I was wondering about how it connected with
what he'd let slip yesterday, as we got into the limo and
the ferry bumped into the dock and came to a halt and
everybody started their engines, and then the big door

opened like a sea monster's mouth and we filed out and
were back on the road.

It was lusher than Newfoundland here, but there was
just as much of it. We didn't talk all the way across Cape
Breton because I was reading the brochures, and once
we were over the Canso Causeway and onto the main-
land we passed all sorts of small towns, if the road signs
were anything to go by, but we didn't see any of the
towns themselves because we were on the Trans
Canada. I counted three dead porcupines before Truro
and then the road climbed over the spine of Nova Scotia
to a toll booth, and Grady of course didn't have any
change on him, so I dug out $2.50 from my bag.

"First they make us use the highway and then they
charge us for it. Bloody capitalists," said Grady, in a
Russian accent.

We started going down the other side of the province
and onto some rolling land, grassier with redder soil.

I looked at a sign. "Amherst," it said, "Next three
exits," and I sighed. "I'm bored again, Grady."

"In Amherst? That's impossible. Amherst is the gate-
way to...well, anywhere else than Amherst. But if you
want excitement, you'll have to go to Moncton."

And there it was again, so I figured I might as well
follow the clues. "Why? What's there?"

"What *isn't* there in Moncton?" said Grady, and he
started singing.

> "The tidal bore, oh the tidal bore
> If you want something, we got more

Magnetic Hill, Magnetic Hill...
It's all there in Moncton..."

It was his BS voice still, but you could tell he wanted me to get interested.

"Is it really Moncton where the tidal bore is?"

"Wanna go see it?" he said, kind of fast.

"Why not? It's gotta be more exciting than this highway." And I watched his eyes to see his reaction.

"Yeah. Sure," he said and he blinked and straightened up in his seat. "We're ahead of time, anyway," though we weren't. "And it'll be the last chance to see salt water for a while..."

He was just rambling, and now I knew for sure he had something up his sleeve.

"Sounds good," I said, waiting for it.

"...And while we're there," he said like it just occurred to him, "I could go see an old friend at the theatre about some business."

So obviously he'd been meaning to go to Moncton and was looking for an excuse to make the stop there seem like it was what *I* wanted.

We crossed into New Brunswick over a low hummock in the flat marsh, past a lone piper in a kilt squealing away in the parking lot of an information centre and a half hour later we took the first exit to Moncton and drove right to the centre of town where we pulled up by a brick sidewalk next to a brass lamp post. There was a small park between two hotels where you could go see the Tidal Bore, and a sign that said the next one was 7:34 that evening, in two hours' time.

Grady said, "I'll go see Matt at the theatre. You can come with me, or if you want to check out the sights, that's okay too, and we can meet back here."

But it was obvious that he didn't want me with him, so I said, "No, Grady. I can entertain myself by studying the architecture and layout of this unique and charming francophone community." I'd been reading the brochures.

"Ah," he said. "And be sure to drink in the delightful ambiance and joie de vivre of the Acadian people."

He went off to the theatre and I walked up the main drag to where the street dipped under a railway, and on the way back I saw, on the opposite sidewalk, a banjo player with his instrument case open in front of him, though nobody was passing. He was wearing little cymbals on his knees, a clown shirt and pants, a great floppy hat, and an expression on his face like he was in Hell. He didn't sound nearly as good as Grady, either, because actually, Grady's not a bad performer, it's just his songs that suck.

I got back to Tidal Bore Park thinking that they must get sick of jokes about the name. The sign at the park said that in French it was called "Le Mascaret," which was a lot better, even a bit exotic.

> Red mud river banks
> wrinkled like an old man's lips
> in French, "Mascaret."

But that haiku wasn't much more than description, and all that last line did was show off that I knew a

French word. So I ripped it out of my notebook and chucked it.

Then I saw Grady coming down the street. "Waiting for the Bore?" he said.

"I think he just showed up."

"You're getting wittier every day, Thea." But you could see that there was something else he wanted to tell me, and sure enough, "Listen..." he started.

"Yes, Grady?"

"I was just talking to that guy I was telling you about? Matt? At the theatre?" Like he was listing just one of the many truthful details he always lays out clearly to keep me filled in with each and every one of our plans so that everybody knows exactly what's happening at all times.

"Yeah?"

"Well, apparently the opening act for the show tonight has dropped out, and they need somebody to fill in."

"It was lucky we happened by," I said, and he looked at me like maybe I was being sarcastic, but I played it straight, so he couldn't tell.

"Anyhow," he said, "If you got nothing better to do...?"

"Go ahead and do your show, Grady."

"OK! Great! Well, that's settled, then. Wanna come see me?"

"No thanks. I want to see the tidal bore."

He was happy now, so he looked at me all mock-horrified. "Oh my God, Thea. I didn't realize that it had come to that."

"I want to *see* it, Grady," I said, so he didn't push it. Then he said he was late for his sound check, and got his guitar out of the trunk and said, "See you after the show, then? Around ten, say?"

"Ten sharp. Here."

"Okay."

And he walked off back to the theatre.

I got into the limo and read some Blake and wrote another three haiku, none of them any good, and pretty soon it was time, so I got out and walked to the park. Four other people were down beside the river now and at first we were all trying not to look embarrassed that there was so little going on in our lives that we had to come to watch this, but then this little guy showed up with an old geezer who must have been his grandfather, and it was probably one of those things that little guys get into their heads that they just have to see, and then grandparents promise them, and then it becomes like it was going to be the greatest thing in their life so far. The kid was nearly peeing his pants.

I mean, here I was thinking that this is probably gonna suck, but then when I looked at him I wished I could be that enthusiastic about *anything* anymore.

He was singing parts of a song in French.

« *Est-ce qu'on voit la mer, Papa ?*
Est-qu'on voit la mer ?
Ça fait si long
Si bien longtemps ... »

Which I knew from French class, where our teacher once invited a performer from Quebec who was on tour out west, and who got in front of the class and taught us the chorus which we, like, *had* to sing. And at the time I thought, these folksinging nazis, I mean, if I don't want to sing, why should I? But now I'm kind of glad he did teach it to us after all, because now I could understand what the kid was singing about, though when they started to talk to each other I was lost.

Then, around the corner of the river I saw this wrinkle in the river which couldn't be anything else, and I guess I must know some French after all because I said, "Voilà!" and I got a loud voice, so everybody heard me, and then Grandad picked up the kid and put him on his shoulders and pointed downriver where this dead straight line from shore to shore was moving up against the current, looking completely unnatural, like a thin carpet rolled up by invisible hands. As it got closer you could start to hear it going shush-shush like one long never-ending wave, not the kind on the seashore with another wave behind to push it along, but all alone, crawling up the current slowly, stirring the river back into itself, rolling right past us red and muddy, and once it passed the water behind was higher by about a foot.

It was thrilling. And the kid was jumping up and down and clapping his hands and Grandad was just as pleased as could be, like he'd arranged it for him, which he had, kind of. They were smiling away, looking around to see if anybody else had seen it, and so was I. Made me want to check out the Magnetic Hill.

We smiled at each other some more, but I couldn't say anything else, so they moved away and I left the bank of the river and went back to the limo to nap and when it was time I went over to the theatre to wait for

Grady who was probably finished his part of the show by then. I went up to the lady who took the tickets.

"How's the crowd?" I asked.

"Pretty good," she said. And I looked over where there was a poster taped to the wall of Chuck T. Boggs, the star of the show, who looked like a total yahoo.

Glued at an angle below was a smaller poster where somebody had written with a marker "With Special Guest, Grady Jordan!" showing Grady walking down a railway.

"I was wondering if I could have that poster," I said. "Now that you won't need it any more, I mean."

"You'd have to ask their management," she said and she left the booth and went over and talked to somebody hanging around the merchandise table who came over.

"Ten Bucks," he said. "Twenty if you want it signed."

"I meant the Grady Jordan poster."

"Oh, that? Yeah, sure, kid. Get it out of my sight. It's been bothering me ever since I first saw it."

"Oh?" I said. "How long you had it hanging here?"

———•‖••‖•———

Grady got a room as part of the deal, but I told him that I'd sleep in the limo.

"Jeez Thea. I wasn't thinking. If I'd known I woulda negotiated a suite."

"This afternoon?"

"What?"

"You would have negotiated a suite this afternoon? When you cut that deal with Chuck T Boggs?"

"What? Oh. Yeah."

But I let it slide. "That's all right," I said. "I like sleeping in the limo. My stuff's all there."

So Grady drove the limo around and parked in the big lot behind the hotel and we set a time to meet for breakfast, and I went up to his room and took a bath with all the hair gels and shampoos and soaps I could find then came down and crawled into the back of the limo and into my sleeping bag where I read the Book of Revelations in my stolen bible until I started to scare myself, then went to sleep, wishing I had a cat to keep me company.

I woke up early and went to the park to see another mascaret, but it wasn't as good as the day before, or maybe now I was just jaded. The sun was coming up and everything was golden, but there was no hyper kid cheerleading this time. Nobody else at all around that early, so I went back and slept for another two hours and then met Grady for breakfast.

5

Murmurings of Revolt

After The Big To-do at school, Mom got the brilliant idea that she'd teach me herself, so she applied for permission to home-school me. She was trained as a teacher anyway, before she came to the conclusion that the education system is garbage. Which is true. But Mom's course turned out to be a total disaster as well.

In the morning she'd start in on World Spirituality and Finger Painting, then in the afternoon Numerology and Sense-Awareness. So I figured if I didn't want to end up an airhead I'd better bone up on something solid, like poetry.

And learning on my own was a lot better. It's because once you find somebody you like you can check out whoever *they* like, and one thing links up with another until eventually you know everything. But because you're feeling your way through bit by bit, it all makes sense as you go, not like school where you jump around from one subject to another and nothing means anything.

For instance, I was getting into Blake because Russell liked him, and then I started on anybody else he or they liked, and that's how I found out about Russell's friends, like the philosopher GE Moore, who Russell claims was the most honest man he ever knew. In fact, the only way he ever got Moore to tell a lie he says was by asking Moore whether he had ever told a lie, and when Moore said that yes he had, Russell said he believed that was the only lie Moore had ever told. It's the same sort of logic as his paradox.

Still, I thought, it would be nice to be around people like that who you could just take at their word and not have to decipher everything they said to find out what their real agenda. You can trust Mom to say what she believes. The problem is that what she does believe is almost always questionable, though she's sincere about it. And Grady's got more of a clue about how things actually work, sort of, but you never know if what he's saying is just to get you to do what he wants.

And I get why. Because people are always trying to get you to do what *they* want, so if you tell the truth all the time, you're just giving them the advantage.

Also, who says honesty really is the best policy? Russell and his friends were into it, trying to construct a view of the world you could hang onto, but what if you do that all your life and it ends up with a paradox? You could have been having fun the whole time and robbing a bank when you needed the money, instead of, like, examining the nature of reality.

We were driving up what the brochures called "The French Shore of New Brunswick" with the sun on my shoulders on a straight two-lane, headed north over shallow hills, then down and across another river with a glimpse of the ocean at its mouth.

I looked at the map and there was another road that wound around the coast, but Grady said it would take too long, so I figured I'd just watch what was in front of me.

Interesting is
About being interested.
Look around you. Now.

Which was a haiku that was definitely getting somewhere, though it kind of sounded like something Mom would say in one of her Universal Awareness classes.

We filled up with gas and paid more than in Gander, so back on the road Grady said, "They're raising the price again. Man! These people!"

"Who?"

"Big Oil. And they owe *me* money!"

"How?"

"I performed for one of their conventions last month and they didn't pay me..." then he paused, slapped the steering wheel and said, "Damn!"

"What?"

"It wasn't them at all! It was Beaumont!"

"Who?"

"My management. They just took the money and blamed them!"

"Who's Beaumont?"

"Gordon Beaumont? Reclusive rich guy? You must've heard of him."

"You just said he's reclusive."

"Yeah, but he's famous."

"How does *that* work?"

He wiggled his fingers like sprinkling magic dust. "Showbiz, Thea. Dazzle 'em, then move in and pick their pockets."

"Looks like they just picked yours."

"I know!"

"So why are you still with them?"

"I'm not, really... It's all up in the air right now..."

A possibility occurred to me. "Grady," I said. "Is this limo still Beaumont's?"

"What..? No...It *was*...but...no... I won it off Chuck T, like I told you..."

"Chuck T Boggs?"

"Yes."

"Who you opened for last night?"

"The same."

"You never told me it was Chuck T you won it off."

"Didn't I? Oh. Well. It was."

"And how'd Chuck T get it off Beaumont?"

"It was... He...Chuck T... musta got it off... or won it... or something... I don't know.... Anyhow... It's ours now. Don't worry about it..."

With such an ironclad explanation as that, how could I ever doubt he was hiding anything?

◆-┤┼┈┼┼-◆

We got to some place that was called "Newcastle" on our old map, but "Miramichi" on the sign on the way into town, and Grady said we'd missed the road around and we'd have to go through town now, which I didn't mind because if you don't get off the highway from time to time, all you see are gas stations.

So we crossed a river and turned onto a smaller road past some strip malls and parking lots and asbestos-shingled houses with boat trailers in yards and moose antlers over shed-doors.

Then just as we were starting to get back into countryside the road took us beside a pulp mill, and I mean "dark satanic" just about perfectly described it, with a mountain of scarred logs like piles of war dead in front of a chimney billowing smoke, and a fifteen-foot-high chain-link fence with three strands of barbwire on top, to stop anybody from sneaking in to bask in the loveliness of the surroundings, I guess.

"What's that smell?" I said.

"Ah, Thea," said Grady, and he breathed in deep like getting a big healthy lungful. "Why, that's the Smell of Prosperity."

"Prosperity smells like a fart?"

"Good one, Thea. But that's what people say, anyway."

"Really?"

"Yeah. Because when you smell that, see, it means that the mill hasn't closed down and your father still has a job."

"Because you can't have both, right? Clean air and a job?"

"You're not supposed to ask that."

And maybe I shouldn't have been reading the Book of Revelations the night before, because I had a sharp and clear vision of Hell...

Then a small bird bounced off our windshield and I snapped out of it.

━┼━┼━

At Renous we turned onto the road that would take us across the province and up ahead there were three native guys who waved us down, and Grady said, "Uh-oh, what's this?" and he stopped and powered down the window as one of them came over and said they were trying to raise money for an "anti-fracking" demonstration. So I dug into my bag for a couple of loonies and handed them to Grady who handed them to the guy who said, "Have a nice day. Meegwitch." And Grady said, "Good luck with it," and powered up the window and drove off.

"The natives are restless," he said.

"That's pretty racist."

"Why?" he said, genuinely curious.

I could never get a rise out of Grady with race, though with Mom it's almost too easy. For instance, there was this guy in my class, Jimmy Fisher, who came over to our place once and Mom starts paying a lot of attention to him, and at first I think it's because she thinks he's my boyfriend, which he's not, but then I figure out that it's because he's native, and the reason she's practically doing back-flips in the kitchen is she's actually got

an honest-to-god indigenous person in the house. So I get
Jimmy out of there before she asks him to do a war-
dance or something. "Sorry about Mom," I said to him
when we were outside.

"That's cool, Thea," he said. "Didn't you know? All
whites are racist."

I thought for a bit. "That's a pretty racist thing to say,"
I said, and he laughed, so that was okay.

The thing is, though, Mom isn't against natives, just
the opposite, but she certainly treated Jimmy differently
than if he was white, which means she's at least
race-*conscious*, anyway.

But racism is such a lot of BS, just stupid categorical
thinking, sets and subsets. I mean, of course there's no
difference between people. We're *all* idiots.

Over the next hill I saw down in the valley a bunch of
cars with flashing lights, and a crowd of people, and as
we got closer we saw more natives, one of them in full
ceremonial regalia holding a warrior flag, and as we got
closer we heard drums drumming and people chanting.

There were also some cops hanging around posing,
talking to each other like it was business as usual, though
you could tell they were more than usually alert, eyes
darting around under casual lids, thumbs in their waist-
bands, one hand never far from their holsters, ready to
draw. Cowboys and Indians.

And what they were all posing for, were the cameras,
two media trucks with satellite dishes on their rooves to
beam out live coverage of whatever was going to happen.

Grady starts to slow down and then says in a voice
like a British bobby, "Ello 'ello'. What's all this then?"

And we roll to a halt behind two other cars, and it doesn't look like we're going anywhere for a while, so we both step out to look around.

Grady asks a cop, "What's going on?" And the cop says, "It's a protest," which we'd both already figured out, thanks.

"Oh?" says Grady. "What about?"

"I can't comment on that, sir," says the cop.

So I say, "Why not?"

He looks at me, then looks back at Grady, even though I was the one who'd asked. "Orders," he says.

"That's not an answer," I say. "Whose orders?" And both Grady and the cop look at me now.

"Sorry Miss," says the cop. "I'm not at liberty to tell."

Which is total BS. I mean, I'm sure he hasn't been instructed that he must under no circumstances divulge any information about where his orders are coming from.

"Come on, Thea," says Grady, taking my wrist.

But I shake him off. "No," I say. "I want to know. But I guess I'll have to go ask somebody who has a clue." And I turn and walk over toward two native guys who are holding some handbills.

"Sorry about that," I hear Grady say to the cop, and I know that the cop is still looking at me, checking me out like his massive computer brain is analyzing whether I'm a possible terrorist threat, but he's still just posing, you can tell. And I look back at him once, like, so? And when he sees I'm looking, he looks over at the license number of the limo and he whips out his phone, like, 'draw!' and types it in. Then he looks back at me like I'd better watch it if I knew what was good for me.

One of the native guys sees everything, and I walk over to him and he says hi and asks me whether I want one of his handbills and I say sure and he hands me one and I ask, "What's it about?"

"They want to start fracking here, and we say that they should 'frack off', and go 'frack themselves'" Then he smiles and says, "Pretty well beat that joke to death, haven't we?"

"What's fracking"? I say.

"They take petroleum from underground shale by injecting water at high pressure. Follow?"

"Do I look retarded?" I say. I guess I was still angry at the cop.

He takes a small step back and looks me up and down. "The footwear might raise some suspicions," he says.

And I had to smile, because he was referring to my boots, which I think are dead cool, but which other people do tend to find a bit strange.

"They were a gift." I say, though they weren't.

"Ah, relatives," he says. "Thank God we can choose our friends."

"You got that right."

"Anyway, where was I?"

"Fracking."

"Oh Yeah. Well, it screws up the ground water."

"So why do it?"

His angry friend moved closer and snorted. "Because they are a giant corporation who doesn't care about anything but money. I mean, we've tried to play by the rules, but supposing the people who make the rules have

only one rule? That they can do whatever they want?
Okay? So you move, and then they come in and screw
up your groundwater and then there's no place to move
to? What then, eh? Move? *Again...?*"

I didn't know why he was asking me.

"...I mean, we've lived here since like, forever, mind-
ing our business, and some fat cat wants to charge us for
bottled water, sold from stores they own, which we have
to pay for with money we make from working for crap
wages at the plant they own, just to get some water to
drink, because the river's polluted now thanks to them. I
mean...you can only back up so far...."

The first guy was looking at him, worried, and he
broke in.

"...And they would certainly get away with it," he said,
"if it weren't for fourteen brave natives handing out flyers
in Matnagut, New Brunswick." He pronounced it "Noo
Bruns Vick" and clicked his heels with a little nazi salute.

The angry guy moved off to give somebody else a
handbill and an earful. As he left it felt like backing away
from a bonfire into the cool night air behind.

The first guy looked at the limo. "Nice wheels," he
said. "You movie stars?"

"That's us." I said. "Grady Jordan's my dad."

"Really?"

"Yeah. Ever hear of him?"

"No."

"Well, don't worry," I said. "Nobody has. I think he's
hoping the limo will help with that."

"You never know."

"You never do," I said, which sounded like a good exit line, I gestured with the handbill. "Meegwitch," I said.

"Hey!" he said, "It's starting to catch on!"

So I walked back to the limo where Grady was sitting with the door open and his feet out on the ground, looking at the map. "I suppose we could take the Doaktown Road," he said, "but it means more time…"

I slid into the passenger's seat, and then there was a loud noise in front of us, and we both looked up. "Wait," he says. "Something's happening…"

I look out the windshield as the chanting starts to speed up and the guys with the cameras move forward and start taping. A different cop than the first comes over and says, "Maybe you should turn back…" and there's another noise that everybody turns to look at, and then the car ahead of us starts up and the cop says, "Wait… they seem to be letting you through," as the two cars in front of us move forward on a signal from somebody we couldn't see, and Grady swings his legs inside and closes the door and starts the engine, and we follow onto the gravel shoulder.

And just as we're squeezing through the last part of the crowd, Grady by mistake spins his tires and sends some gravel flying behind, and somebody yells "Hey!" and thumps the hood of the trunk, and I think, that's pretty rude, but Grady gets the limo back onto the pavement where the road is open in front of us, and he guns it out of there.

I turn in my seat and look behind and see the crowd starting to squirm like water before it comes to a boil. And as we're moving away I see somebody push a cop as a native lady grabs hold of a cop's arm and falls down, and like that! a spring trips and everybody is fighting and pushing and kicking and falling, everything getting smaller in the distance behind us, and the very last glimpse I get is of a real battle going on now as we go over a hill and then it was gone, snatched away from me.

"Let's go back, Grady."

"I don't think so."

"Why not?"

"It's getting ugly."

"The one part of the trip that's not boring, and you run away from it!"

"No Thea. That's final."

But since when did he have the right to tell me any-thing? I mean, me and Mom hadn't heard from him since I was fourteen years old, so for a quarter of my life he hadn't been around at all, and before that he was occa-sionally there, but by no means always.

"I got that poster of you from the theatre, Grady," I said.

"What? Oh. Really?"

"Yes."

"So... What, then? Would you like me to sign it for you?"

"No, Grady. I would not like you to sign it for me." And then he knew something was up. "The guy at the merchandise table said that he was sick of seeing it."

"Norman? He's an idiot. Backstage last night the crew they told me that he once..."

"Don't change the subject, Grady. I mean, it's a bad poster all right, but it probably wouldn't make you sick of seeing it after only three hours."

"I don't understand...."

"He told me that it had been up for a few weeks."

"They must've...had some from when I played there before."

"Oh? And they put it up three weeks before, hoping that you'd just happen by on the day of the show?"

"That was maybe because..."

"You knew you were going to do that show, Grady. So why all this pretending you were taking me to see Moncton?"

"You liked Moncton didn't you? You thought the tidal bore was great, didn't you?"

I didn't say anything.

"Look," he said. "Nobody's on this road now. How about if I teach you how to drive?"

"What do I want to know how to drive for?"

"It's fun."

"I don't care, Grady."

"Come on, Thea. Everybody wants to know how to drive."

"Not me."

"Why not?"

"Why should I?"

"Because you should."

"That's not a reason. And you're doing it again."

"What?"

"You're trying to distract me, and making it sound like you're doing it for me, but you just want to get to your next show and you figure you might need some help driving."

"You're just being foolish now."

"Oh? Well then, what did you mean when you said that you'd get the money together for the flight somehow?"

"What?"

"Before we came into Port Aux Basques."

"I don't remember..."

"I had you scared that I was turning into a religious maniac and you said if I wanted we could go back to St John's and you'd raise the money for the ticket somehow."

"You must've misheard," he said. But I just crossed my arms and kept looking at the side of his face until he looked back over. "No, I mean, look, Thea. I just meant that I... I don't know, I..."

"Did you mean that you didn't have the money for the ticket because you'd cashed it in already?"

"No, I..."

"You *did* mean that, didn't you?"

"No...I..."

Then it occurred to me why he'd done it. "To get into that game of cards!" I said. "That was it, wasn't it, Grady? You cashed in my ticket to have the money to get into a game of cards!"

"Look. Thea..."

"It's true, isn't it?"

"No...I..."

"How much money do we have?

"Enough."

"How much exactly?"

"Let me explain. We needed some money for the trip..."

"So you admit it! You did cash in my ticket!"

"Not like you make it sound..."

"You sold back my ticket to bet on a limo for your lame little tour!"

"I thought it would be a good way to get to know each other..."

"Oh I'm getting to know you all right. You're a liar and a crook. You might have stolen this limo for all I know."

"I didn't!"

"But you could be lying about that too, couldn't you? Is that it? Did you, like, steal this limo?"

"No way, Thea."

"Prove it."

"There's the pink slip under the visor. Look at it if you want."

But the fact that he was saying that probably meant that he actually did have one, so I didn't check it out, because if it was true I would have to admit that I was wrong about that, and he'd say "see," like that proved I was accusing him falsely about everything. So, as with almost everything to do with Grady, I put it in the "maybe" file, feeling like Bertrand Russell figuring out some mathematical problem by having to hold this whole structure of "if-then" statements in his head, and wishing I could just blow it all away like Blake with a sudden blinding vision that took everything into account and nailed it once and for all.

So I gave him the silent treatment.

He'd say "Look Thea..." and I just wouldn't answer, and an hour later he'd try to break the silence and say something else, and I'd just ignore him.

And I didn't say a word all the way up to Plaster Rock between those phony "beauty strips" to New Denmark where they bury their barns, then onto the highway and into the Province of Quebec past St Louis-de-ha!-ha! and over into the St Lawrence Valley, down to La Pocatière where the road goes right by the water. For more than five hours I threw a chill over everything. I started to understand how Mom did it.

6

Showbiz

By the time we passed Montmagny I was ready to say something, but Grady broke the silence first.

"I'm sorry Thea," he said. "But this is kinda stupid, isn't it?"

"You couldn't have just, like, told me the truth?"

"I thought if I did, you wouldn't come along with me."

"Boo hoo. And why *should* I come along with you if you're a lying two-faced cheat?"

"I dunno what to say, Thea..."

"Oh yeah, play it for sympathy, like you're the victim. What else do you have planned? Tell me."

"I gotta go meet someone in Ottawa, because that's where I pick up the cheque for last night."

"You didn't get paid for last night?"

"Not yet. So we gotta get to Ottawa. And we will. I promise."

"Oh yeah, like I'm going to believe your promises!"

"We're on our way to Prince Rupert, aren't we?"

"Not how I thought we would."

"Still. We're getting there. And I'm...trying."

"Not hard enough."

"Well... I've been going through some... hard times lately... But we'll get the money, I promise."

"Ha!"

"I mean, if the price of gas stays this high, we'd *better* get it..."

I looked at him. "We don't have enough money?"

"We should be okay, but don't worry. We'll be fine..."

"How?"

"Well...I was thinking maybe you could phone your mother..."

"No!"

"Why not?"

"I don't know whether you *heard*, but she doesn't want anything to *do* with you, Grady."

"Yeah, but if *you* ask?"

"No."

"Well what do you want me to do, then?"

"How much money do you have?"

He dug out his wallet from under his butt and held it on the steering wheel with one hand and thumbed it open, glanced inside then did a double take. "Why, that *is* getting a bit low," he said, like he was surprised.

"How much?"

"Twenty dollars."

"Give it here."

"But..."

"Give. It. *Here*."

"Okay okay okay. Take it. And don't worry. It's more than enough to get us to Ottawa."

I took out the roadmap, looked at the distance chart and calculated. The limo took about ten dollars of gas every hundred klicks, which meant that the twenty dollars Grady had just given me and the five I had with me would get us as far as (I looked at the map) some place called St. Hyacinthe, doubtless a dreamy little village with a big silver-rooved Quebec church surrounded by old growth maple woods which would be perfect for hiding Grady's body after I murdered him.

I looked ahead as we passed Exit 38 then back at the map. "Take the next exit, Grady."

"What?"

"Take a right. Here. Get off the Highway. Now! I'm serious!"

He took the exit and came to the T at the end.

"Follow the signs to Centre-Ville Lévis," I said.

"But, why?"

"Just do it."

So he drove down to the river right to the ferry wharf where we parked in the lot and got out. Quebec City loomed up across the river. I dug around in my bag for some loonies for the fare.

"I don't know if it's wise to spend the last..."

"Take your guitar," I said.

He popped open the trunk and took it out. "Okay," he said, "but I don't know what you're planning to..."

"We're taking the ferry."

"Did you, like, call somebody?"

"Keep walking."

"But Thea. If you think you're going to like, just rent a concert hall..."

"We're not going to 'rent a concert hall,' Grady. We don't have the money to 'rent a concert hall'."

"Okay, but even getting a job in a bar, you can't just walk in and expect..." He stopped suddenly and drew back. "You're not going to pawn my guitar!"

"No, Grady. I'm not going to pawn your guitar."

"Well what are we doing?"

So I told him, "My friend Marcia is working on a French Immersion Program in a restaurant here, and the last time I called her she mentioned that she was looking for somebody to play the dinner crowd. She told me if you liked you could play there."

He totally bought it. "Really?"

"Yes."

"But. What? She can just get money to..."

"One of her mandates is to dispense money for arts groups."

"Wow. We should definitely get to know her then."

"I already know her, Grady. I told you, she's a friend."

"Well, okay, then. Let's go!" He was like a little kid. "Where is it?"

"You'll see."

Marcia Watkins was not here, of course. She was back in Prince Rupert getting ready to volunteer for Daisy Ratzinger. It was a bald-faced lie I was telling, but I could see the point. It got things done.

The ferry fought the current and docked, we walked onboard, and it shuddered out into the tide pushing up

river. Quebec City sat on top of a big grey cliff in front us,
looming larger and larger as we crossed in an arc against
the current, then the ferry pushed into the wharf and tied
up. A sign said "Basse-ville" with an arrow pointing and I
was thinking we'd walk up the hill to the centre of town,
so we got off the boat and crossed the road toward the
smaller buildings built up around the bottom of the cliff.
It looked like Europe, not that I've ever been there, but
I've seen pictures, and so had they too, I guess. All a bit
too much like the tourist brochures, if you want my
opinion, though maybe I only thought that because I was
feeling extremely angry at everything right now, thank
you.

We came to a square with a few restaurants around
where some steps led up to where I thought we would go,
but then I thought that this might be as good a place as
any.

"Is this the restaurant?" said Grady.

"There is no restaurant, Grady. Now. Take out your
guitar and start playing for the crowd."

"What crowd?"

"Well we have to attract one first, don't we?"

"What? Here?"

"Yep."

"You lied."

"Now you know what it feels like."

He thought for a bit. "Okay," he said. "We're even."

"We are nowhere close to even, Grady. Now. Put the
guitar case down, and open it up."

"Thea..."

"Do it."

"Okay," he said, and he put it down and clicked open the case. "But I'm not gonna..."

"Yes you are. Take the guitar out and hang it around your neck. Leave the guitar case open."

"But..."

"If you don't do what I say I'll go to the police and say that you kidnapped me. I'll say you've been acting all drugged-up, and that you stole this limo. I'll scream. You know I will..." And I opened my mouth.

"Okay okay okay. Jeez Thea...." He took out his guitar and started tuning, and he tuned and re-tuned, and somebody passed, and then somebody else looked and smiled as he passed, and finally somebody stopped, cocked an ear, but then almost immediately moved on.

But Grady wasn't singing or playing, he was just strumming softly and listening to himself, so I went back to him.

He said "This ain't working, Thea..."

"Well of course not if you don't try."

"Ah Thea. This is just not my scene."

"Well you better make it your 'scene' then, hadn't you? Because we're not going anywhere until we have gas money." I took a CD from the guitar case and looked at the back. "Play 'Long Road,'" I said.

Then I dug into my bag and took out the last of my change and threw half of it into the guitar case. I had a vision that it was like casting seeds onto the ground, and that these few coins would grow and breed others.

"I don't know if I even remember it."

"Play what you do remember."

So Grady strummed once, strummed twice, and played a run from way up the neck that built into a nice chugging rhythm. I'd only told Grady to do that song because it was the first song I read on the CD cover, but it turned out that it was a pretty good song to start a show, and I guess that's why he'd put it at the start of the disk.

It's a looo-ooooooong road
Don't know where's it's going

A looooooo-ong road
Like some river flowin'...

But people kept passing without throwing money in, so I walked out and stood in front like I'd stopped to listen, to make other people less self-conscious about stopping, but they still kept passing by, so I started to clap along, meekly, like a tourist might who was just getting into it. And I tried to become less self-conscious myself, which is hard to do. I mean, the more you try to be less self-conscious, the less you are able to, because you're conscious of doing that. It's like a paradox.

And now that I was performing too, sort of, I saw what Grady was up against and I almost felt sorry for him. I could see that if you let it get on top of you it could be humiliating. People weren't just passing and not looking, they were passing by and looking at everything *but* him, trying to avoid the embarrassment of catching his eye. And on every face, marks of weakness, marks of woe.

Across the square outside a restaurant there was a nasty-looking waiter leaning on a wall smoking, and it was the type of restaurant that was trying to be as close to what they think tourists would take as an authentic Québécois experience, but I mean, the staff were dressed like peasants, for godsakes. And there was some low volume musical pap coming out of loudspeakers set up on the street. The waiter finished his cigarette and snorted, and went back inside and, what's really rude, he turned up the music.

Grady, who was getting into it now, frowned and played harder, and sung louder but suddenly I felt like I wanted him to just give up.

They've won, I thought. It was like the angry guy at Matnagut had said. Some big faceless corporation had surrounded everybody with only their own music, and if you didn't like it, too bad, better find some other planet to inhabit, because that's what we play here on earth, everywhere, no exceptions. And I started to make plans to call Mom...

And then this drunk came out of the restaurant.

He was wearing an expensive business suit that looked like it'd been slept in, and he staggersed out the door like a stage drunk, knees wobbling every which-way, trying to put on his raincoat by ramming an arm into one sleeve with the other sleeve hanging inside out, and the raincoat itself twisted around on his back with half the lining showing. He's a huge stumbling disaster, but he doesn't care, or is pretending he doesn't, seeing the humour in it himself, rotating at the same time as trying to swat at the tail of the raincoat behind him like it's chasing him. Also one shoelace is undone of course, so he stumbles and bumps softly into someone and says "M'excuse," and then sees Grady like he recognizes him and comes tacking toward him.

"Ti-cul! Joue-moé 'la Danse aux Enchères'...' he says.

And I think that this is going to be a disaster, but Grady sees him coming and doesn't stop playing, just takes it all in stride, and then... *includes* him. He points at him with the head of his guitar and dips down on the beat, and the drunk does the same, dips down himself, just happy to have someone not avoiding him, then makes this pathetic attempt to dance a little two-step with a jump on the end, and when he comes down he lands bad, gets under himself and straightens, and people have to stop now, because he's flinging his arms about to regain his balance. Which he does, then puts this dopey expression on his face like it was all a planned performance.

And the people who have stopped there, all smile because they see he's harmless, and he bows deeply with his fingers spread across his chest, and nearly falls over again, so everybody applauds him and he walks away with a swagger, and Grady finishes up the tune like it was all part of the performance, and I go forward and drop my last loonies into his guitar case, and some guy does the same, and then two or three others.

And then the song on the speakers comes to an end, and a new one doesn't start, I guess because it looks like Grady'll be good for business now, and Grady starts in on song number two. And once he's into it, Grady doesn't suck. I gotta say, I was impressed.

He played there for two hours, and sometimes it worked and sometimes it didn't, but he didn't give up till a cop came and closed us down. He asked whether we had "un permis", and Grady said "Non", and so we had to move on, which was fine because when I counted the money we had more than enough to get us to Ottawa.

On the way back across the river the boat was arcing with the current in the opposite direction from when we'd come, pulling down river now. The tide had turned.

—‖··‖—

"Forty-two bucks," I said. We were back on the road and I was counting the money again. "I should be your manager."

He paused and thought. "Jeez, Thea, I'd love that."

"Really?"

"Why not?"

I considered. "What would I do?"

"Find some talented sucker and rip him off."

"Talented, eh? Guess I'm out of luck there."

"Ouch."

"Seriously, Grady. How'd you get that gig in Moncton, for instance?"

"It was my last show for Beaumont. I was wrapping up my contract with them."

"But you said they didn't pay you in St. John's. So why would you even agree to do it?"

"Didn't have a manager."

"Okay."

"Also I hadn't yet figured out that they were the ones who ripped me off. And we were coming this way anyway..."

"Were we really?"

"I'm sorry I didn't make it more clear, Thea."

"It wasn't that you didn't 'make it more clear,' Grady. You lied to me. Why?"

"Force of habit?" he said. Which sounded honest, anyway.

"Well, who needs those jerks anyway?" I said. "Why don't you just play your songs on the street? You should be able to at least earn a living."

"I suppose..."

"See, Grady, maybe your problem is that you want to be a 'star', whatever *that* is."

"Didn't realize you thought about it so much, Thea."

"The crew from 'The Celebrities' were up in Prince Rupert last year."

"Really?"

"Yeah, and I mean, what a bunch of posers. Jimmy Fisher, this guy I know, he was on the show."

"Lucky him."

"I don't know how lucky it was. Jimmy's got a pretty good voice, see, and the AV class made a video of one of his songs for the amateur show, and somebody sent it to them and these posers from The Celebrities phone him up and tell him that he's been selected for their competition, though it turns out they're only doing that because he's like, part Tl'ingit, and they want to cash in on some tax-break for hiring aboriginals, which must make *him* feel real special about his singing talent. I mean who cares what category he is, if he can sing? Anyhow, when they phone him he says he'd love to, and then tells everybody at school that he's just using them to get what he wants, trying to stay cool. But I mean now he's going to be on the lamest show on TV.

Everybody watches it, though, and he does okay, too, although he looks nervous. And then he's standing there being criticized by people who, like, the best thing they've ever done is this crappy show. The only reason we watch it is to say what garbage it is, which is kinda sick, when you think about it. So I don't watch TV anymore."

"You're not missing much."

"I know."

Before coming into Montreal we saw from the distance the skyline and the mountain with the cross on it, the buildings higher than the cross, and the telecommunications tower higher than either, which should tell you something.

Then we went under the river in a tunnel, and out and around back of the mountain, with a big domed church which for some reason Grady called "Joe's Place," and then onto an elevated road and a freeway with heavy traffic between warehouses and malls, where there must've been an airport because a big plane flew low over the highway in front of us, looking like it was going to land slow-motion on somebody's roof.

By the time we got back into countryside it was late and we were still about an hour and a half from Ottawa, but Grady said he was tired so we pulled into a rest area with a *cantine mobile* parked across from the washrooms, and I thought I might shoplift something to eat, but it looked like a family operation, so it wouldn't be right, although if you thought about it, that didn't make any logical sense. We had some money now anyhow though, so we bought ourselves a microwaved chicken pot pie, which we ate at a picnic table.

"The crust," I said. "It tastes like cardboard."

"Now, now, Thea. Be fair. If you notice, there is also a distinct hint of gyprock dust."

"Oh wait. It *is* cardboard. I was eating the paper plate."

"Probably more nutrition, anyway."

"Good point. I might have seconds."

"Waitress, a few more paper plates, s'il vous plaît."

"With a side order of boiled napkins."

We were both smiling.

"It's like some of Mom's meals," I said.

"Come on now. Your mom's a fine cook."

"Yeah, mostly. But every now and then she loses it completely. Like last spring she read something about seaweeds that are supposed to cure everything, and we were eating anything she was raking up from the shore and some of it was pretty rank."

I looked at his face and it was like he was thinking about Mom and smiling, and I gotta admit that I thought then that maybe they could get back together and we'd be one big happy family, like in some garbage Hollywood movie. Then I thought that I should try and keep it real and like Mom would say, just enjoy the moment.

"How'd you get into showbiz, Grady?"

"It was after University in Newfoundland."

"I didn't know you went to university."

"Well, it wasn't one of the great academic careers of all times," he said, then grinned at me. "Though, amongst other things, I did learn what a haiku is, of course."

"I figured. Even for you, that sounded too stupid."

"Just messing with you."

"So what did you take?"

"At college? Folklore."

"Why that?"

"That's where the best guitar players were."

"So why aren't you, like, a professor or something?"

"I believe it had something to do with The Great Tilley's Pond Disaster..."

"Okay," I said, "what happened?" Because you could see he was itching to tell about it.

"I'm glad you asked. It was when I went out collecting songs..."

"Collecting what?"

"Songs."

"How do you do *that?*"

"Find some people who know a bunch and record them. Anyhow, they gave me the name of a guy named Art Cheadle, who apparently knew thousands, so one fine evening I drove way the hell out around the Bay to Tilley's Pond and when I get there it's a beautiful evening, sea-breeze wafting in from the ocean, smell of cooking from the kitchen, shaping up to be a classic Newfoundland moment, like one of those tourism ads. But nobody answers when I knock on his door, so I walk around behind his house and he's sitting in the doorway of his shed, staring at a shotgun in his hand like he was trying to make up his mind about whether to blow his brains out.

"So (like you would) I ask him whether he'd like to sing some songs for me, and he looks at me like, 'Could you have come at a worse time?' then breathes out like he's made up his mind, and says, 'Got any booze?'

"So I get a bottle of rum from the car and Art slugs back a good quarter of it, wipes his sleeve across his mouth and says, 'That's the first drink I've had in thirty-five years.'"

"And it occurs to me that giving him the booze maybe hadn't been the brightest idea, but Art starts acting like it's the best thing that's ever happened to him. 'Now,' he says, 'Where's that goddamned accordion'? and he goes inside and comes back out with this wheezy piece of crap with no notes on it anywhere near in tune, and takes another belt and starts telling me that his wife has just left him with the priest who's been keeping him sober, and his children, who hate him like poison, were trying to get him locked up in a mental institution so they could sell his house, and it's like the saddest story in the world, but not as sad as this absolute wrist-slitter of a dirge he starts to sing called 'The Blue Eyes of Janey the Belle,' which has like four hundred verses, all of them more pathetic than the one before, and I swear to God he's just making some of it up, because a lot of it, like about forty verses in the middle for instance, are starting to cross over into his own personal story. And the recorder has almost run out of tape by the time it's over, and Art is well into his Sobriety Recovery Program by now, belting back the rum, top of the world till finally his mood crashes, and he's staring into the distance again.

"And then I smell smoke, and there's a fire in the kitchen."

"Oh no."

"Yep. Because he's left his cooking on, and I run in and it turns out it's quite a big fire, actually, so I come screaming out again like 'Where's the fire extinguisher!' And Art says, 'Got none,' quite unconcerned about it all. And I say, 'Phone! Where's the phone!?' And he says, 'Got none, either. Got nothing,' then gets up and walks away and turns and stands there watching his house in flames, and says in this empty voice, 'Burn, you bastard. Right to the ground. Let's see the youngsters sell *that.*'

"And by this time some people from the village start showing up, though no way was there going to be a bucket line or anything, because by now the fire was too big to get anywhere near."

"So I say. 'Okay well, I'd better be off. Thanks for everything,' and I leave, feeling pretty guilty about it all, though it wasn't really my fault, and thinking that at least we got 'The Blue Eyes of Janey the Belle' preserved for posterity. And I write up the paper and my supervisor says, 'That was Art Cheadle you recorded. What we were looking for was some songs from *Arch* Cheadle, his cousin.' So that's why your father isn't Professor Grady Jordan."

"What do you mean that it wasn't really your fault?" I said. "If you hadn't showed up he wouldn't have burnt his house down."

"I figured if I hadn't showed up he woulda blown his brains out."

"I suppose," I said.

"But here's the sequel. Years pass and I find myself playing near Tilley's Cove, and somebody tells me that apparently when his house burned down he went on the bender of all benders, and then, just as he was wallowing in the pit of despair, he received in the mail a moose-hunting license."

"So what?"

"See, he'd always applied for them. In his youth he was quite a well-known hunter apparently, but he never got his license since he was like twenty years old. And suddenly, I don't know, he had a reason to smarten up, maybe? He got his gun and oiled it up and bought some ammunition..."

"Oh boy."

"But it didn't turn out too bad, Thea. As soon as he got that license in the mail he stopped drinking, see. And as surprised as the people of Tilley's Cove were that he ever got that license in the first place, they were more surprised when one crisp day in the fall of the year with one shot he took down a moose, the likes of which had never been seen anywhere near. And he butchered it, quartered it, hauled it back over the frost, four trips, then hung it all in his shed and announced a party, a dry party, for all the people of the church and community to share. I guess he got his pride back with that moose, pulled himself together, and people remarked that he even held himself straighter."

"I see what you're trying to say, Grady..."

"Wait for it. Because the morning of the big do, he went to the shed to get the meat, and he opened the door... and dogs had broken in and ripped the carcasses down and chewed and spoiled all the meat. Not one damned edible mouthful in what had been the best moose ever seen anywhere around."

"Poor guy."

"Yeah, but here's the thing, Thea. Apparently when he found out, he just stood there and looked at the crowd of people he'd invited who were all looking back at him thinking, Oh my God, what's going to happen now? But they never expected what did happen."

"What?"

"Nothing. He never took another drink again, and three years later he hunted and killed another moose, a smaller one, but a moose which he shared with the community, a really nice meal on a really nice evening. And people say there are no heroes left."

"Three years, eh?"

"What?"

"That bender he went on. It lasted three years?"

"That's usually what it takes."

"In your experience?"

But he wasn't ready to talk about it and I didn't push it.

The sun was down now and Grady moved the limo away from the streetlight and arranged himself to sleep in the front seat, complaining about the gear shift sticking into his kidneys, while I stretched out back in perfect comfort and watched through the sunroof the stars appear until I fell asleep.

I woke up hearing him arguing with somebody in a dream.

"You're talking in your sleep, Grady," I said, but he kept babbling. "Grady?" Then, "Dad?" and he stopped and soon I heard him snoring and I went back to sleep feeling good and thinking that the dam had burst and now Grady would tell me whatever I asked.

I mean, how naïve can you get?

7

Politics

We got up at dawn and drove to Ottawa, found a place to park downtown and agreed on a time to meet back at the car. Then Grady popped the trunk and took out his guitar and went to pick up the cheque as I went to look around town.

I walked toward Parliament Hill then into a snazzy hotel where I asked them if I could use their phone. They asked whether I was staying there, and I said yes, room six zero two, and then they asked me if it would be long distance, and I said yes, but I'd call collect and I went to a wall phone and dialed Marcia's number.

Marcia Watkins is my friend from school who lives with her parents who are still together, which is supposed to make her more "emotionally integrated" than me, but I'm not sure. Not that Marcia isn't completely okay and everything, but there's this sort of unspoken assumption that because my parents broke up, I have to be like, permanently scarred or something.

But there are a lot of us around, half the population now, apparently, so it's not like we're out there all alone. And anyhow, I don't see what's the big deal about the so-called "nuclear" family. Sounds radioactive, if you ask me. And if you want my opinion on parents in general, it's that you can have too many of them. I mean, I'm having enough trouble keeping just Grady in line. I don't know if I could handle both Mom and him at the same time.

Not to complain too much about Mom, though. She's okay, I guess, it's just we get sick of each other. During the school-year we're together in Prince Rupert, and when she opened the Café out in Charlotte City in the summer, she's like my boss, which I get, I mean, we need the money and everything, and Mom's always extra careful about letting me do what I have to in my own way, but still it doesn't make it any less irksome.

Most girls I know have problems with their mothers, anyway. Even Marcia is always coming to me with harrowing tales of Mrs. Watkins' embarrassing behaviour, though I think Marcia's mom is pretty cool, frankly, though I don't tell Marcia that because it's almost like she'd be disappointed if she didn't have a Hell-Mom From The Pit. And I know that my mom's not that. It's just people. We get tired of each other.

Anyhow, about Marcia. It was when we were looking for costumes for the beatnik dance, down at the Salvation Army second-hand clothing store, and she's asthmatic, and we're in the back where things are kind of fousty, and first she starts breathing heavy and then she has to sit down, and she takes out her inhaler but it's empty. And then she kind of panics and she's bent over, gasping, and I don't know what to do, and there's nobody in the store for some reason, so I yell, Help! and look into the back room, but there's nobody back there either, and Marcia is gasping and staring at the ground now, her fingernails blue, and then she slumps off the chair onto the floor, and I try to carry her out of the shop, but she's too heavy. So I run out of the store yelling, help! help! help! and it's raining, and I yell to the only person on the street, "Marcia's fallen down in the back of the store!"

But it's Bert, this guy you see around Prince Rupert who doesn't do anything but spend his days just walking around. I mean he must live somewhere, but nobody knows where, and you see him most of the time sipping tea and looking out at the rain. Some guys in school make fun of him, but to me, he's mostly, like, sad.

So I look up the street again for somebody else, but he looks back at me and sees I'm serious, and it's like he *leaps* into action, I mean, superhero time. He sprints into the Sally Ann and comes out with Marcia in his arms like a fireman from a burning building, and he carries her, running, two blocks to the hospital, and they give her an injection, and she's okay.

But here's the thing. Bert has a heart attack and dies. And I go to his funeral with Marcia, and I'm feeling pretty crappy about it, how I wasn't able to help, though every-body's real nice about that, and it's true that if he hadn't saved her, she'd be the one who was dead, and she's sixteen, and he's like a hundred and thirty years old. So I suppose it's more natural that somebody with their whole life in front of them survives rather than some old guy who's only got a few years left anyhow, though it woulda been real nice if, like, both of them lived, so how about that scenario, eh, God? And that was when I started to think that maybe religion was a bit of a sick joke.

And at the funeral Bert's sister comes over and says she wanted to thank us, and I was about to say, for what? Killing your brother? But she saw my face and said, "No. Really. He wouldn't have wanted it any other way." And I thought, well, that's just BS, though of course I didn't say anything, because it's, like, a funeral, and you can't go around calling the mourners a bunch of hypocrites (though a lot of them are).

But it turns out it was true, the way she told it. Bert, see, was from The Czech Republic and he'd come out as a young man and worked at the mill for thirty years and was fired a week before the company had to give him his pension, and he was never very political and had no pull with the union because he'd been on the wrong side of some strike back somewhere, and after he was fired he couldn't get any other work, so he just moped around for like twelve years, walking up and down the hills in Prince Rupert, in the rain, sitting in cafes and muttering into his cup of tea, and what I didn't know was that he used to mention suicide a lot. And when I came out of the Sally Ann screaming about Marcia and he saw me, *that* was the look in his eyes. Suddenly he had something he had to do. But an old guy shouldn't sprint like that with a load like Marcia. And then Bert's sister told me that his last words were, "It was worth it," like the last line in some garbage Hollywood movie, but when I heard it I cried like a baby, and my eyes still well up when I think about it. Like now.

━ ┊┼━┼┊ ━

All to say I was thinking about Marcia as I dialed her number. I wanted to catch up on what was going on, but also there's a show our school puts on every year and I thought I could get Grady to play there. It was like the real version of the lie I'd told to make him cross the ferry to Quebec City.

I dialed and Marcia's mom picked up and accepted the charges.

"Hello Mrs. Watkins. It's Thea. Is Marcia there?"

"No. She's out. But where are you, Thea?"

"Ottawa."

"What are you doing there?"

"Too hard to explain. But don't worry. I'm with Grady."

"How's that supposed to make me not worry?"

"Got a point there, Mrs. Watkins."

"Does your Mom know you're there?"

"Um...no. She thinks I'm still in St John's."

"Why didn't you tell her?"

"She'd have a fit."

"I see. But don't you think you should?"

"I figure that now I've told you, you'll phone her, or you'll tell Bridget and Bridget'll phone her, or at least tell

Emma, who will talk to Wilf and his family and they'll get in touch with his friend... anyhow, word's bound to get back to Mom, that's for sure."

"Are you saying that we're a bunch of gossips, Thea?"

"Hey. It takes a village."

"Good one, Thea. And yes, I'll phone your mom myself. I can't help you with Marcia, though. She's out getting ready for Daisy Ratzinger's campaign, or tour, or whatever it is. Hard to tell the difference."

"I thought you liked her songs."

"I do. The politics are a bit confrontational for my taste, though."

"Well, if you see Marcia, could you tell her I called, then ask her if maybe she can get some work for Grady? He's desperate."

"What's he done now?"

"Nothing specific. Just behaved like Grady."

"I see..."

"But don't worry, Mrs. Watkins. Everything's fine. And tell Mom that everything's fine. I'm fine. Grady's fine. We're all fine."

"Nobody is holding a gun to your head to make you say that?"

"No."

"Mind you, if they were, you wouldn't be able to tell me, would you? So... okay. Answer yes or no, and if the answer is yes, after you hang up tell the people holding a gun to your head that the question I asked you was whether you were eating well. Got it?"

"Okay."

"Good. Now. Is anybody holding a gun to your head?"

"No."

"Good."

"Are you all right, Mrs. Watkins?"

"Sorry. I've been bingeing on movies."

"Okay. Well. Bye, Mrs. Watkins. And say hello to everybody."

"Have fun. And keep that Grady in line."

"Will do."

"Oh! And while you're there in Ottawa. Go see Question Period."

"What's that?"

"House of Commons. Big scandal going on."

"Really?"

"Yep. You can tell Marcia all about it."

"Okay."

"See you in five days, then."

"All right. Bye."

I hung up and felt homesick, but maybe I could see Marcia on the way through British Columbia, where I'd have lots to tell her, and even more after I'd checked out the House of Commons. So I left the hotel and walked up to Parliament Hill, which isn't much of a hill at all, not if you're from Prince Rupert.

I walked by the Cenotaph where they were getting ready for November eleventh, and I passed the "eternal" flame, which as far as I could see was only eternal for as long as the oil supply held out, and where some protesters were holding up signs. Then, beside the big stone staircase at the main entrance seven or eight people were lined up, and I asked a lady what was going on, and she said they were waiting for Question Period, so I lined up

with them until somebody in a uniform opened the door
and we filed into a lobby made of squirrelly rock with a
vaulted ceiling like one of those caverns where the bad
guys in robes stand in a circle and chant near the end of
garbage Hollywood movies. Then I had to check my bag
at the coat-check in case I was trying to smuggle in an
AK-47 or something, and our group joined another longer
line, and we squeezed up against another wall.

I asked an old geezer in front of me, "Is it always this
crowded?"

"Only when the government's in trouble," he said.

"What have they done?"

"You haven't heard?" he said, but not like a put-down.
More like he was happy to get a chance to talk, because
he's, like, ancient, and probably pretty lonely. "The
Prime Minister has been caught in a lie."

In line in front of him there was a jittery guy with red
hair who's not as old as the Geezer, but about thirty-five,
so still pretty old. "Well, that's not necessarily true," he
said. "We shouldn't prejudge."

"You mean like what the PM did with..." and the
Geezer named somebody. "That was different..." said the
Red-Haired Guy, and they were about to get into it, but a
guy in uniform unclicked the velvet rope and we filed up
the hallway, divided into two groups, and were led
through to a balcony with wooden benches looking
down over the floor of the House, a big churchy-looking
room with two banks of pews facing each other.

I took a seat and turned around and saw the Red-
Haired Guy standing there staring at me.

"Could you, like, move over?" he said. "I need that seat."

I looked around and there was nobody else in any of the seats near me, so he was clearly insane, but possibly dangerous as well, so I moved along a few seats toward the Geezer, and the Red-Haired Guy didn't even say thanks but immediately sat down and started shuffling through a sheaf of papers like he was late for something, moving his lips like he was rehearsing lines.

The Geezer saw me looking at him. "There's been a new microphone placement for the visitors," he said. "It's so he'll be picked up by the broadcast," and he pointed at the cameras on the floor of the House.

I had no idea what he was talking about.

Then at the far end of the floor of the House a guy wearing robes stood up and passed it over to the leader of the opposition. And I thought that this was probably going to be pretty boring, and I wondered what Marcia saw in it all.

Then the LEADER OF THE OPPOSITION started talking about Matnagut, and I got interested.

"...Is the reason the Government's bill to allow new chemical deterrents an attempt to further arm the police against these perfectly legal demonstrations?"

He sat, and the people behind him applauded, and in the balcony next to us the Red-Haired Guy craned forward, coughed into his hand and said clearly, but to nobody I could see, "Oh for Godsakes. Let's get on with more important issues, like the economy."

Back on the floor the guy in robes directed the question to the Deputy Prime Minister who stood and said,

"The Right Honourable Leader of the Opposition asked this question yesterday, and the day before..." and he shook his head like he was baffled at how many times he's had to go over it. "...and the Prime Minister has made it abundantly clear on this point...."

Then there were heckles from the Opposition, who started stomping on the floor and snorting, "Since when?" "Get serious!" "Yeah, Right!" and one drunk in the back makes a loud farty noise with his lips, which made everybody laugh. I mean, it was worse than math class with a substitute teacher.

But beside me the Red-haired Guy said to his invisible friend, "No, that's right. He's already answered. Now, let's move on!"

And on the floor of the House the guy in robes stood and said "Order, order...." until the heckling fizzled out. "And Canadians know that pepper spray is a legitimate, effective, and most importantly, *safe* way to control dangerous mob situations, and let me remind you that although thankfully no one was killed in New Brunswick, a police car was burnt, and a whiff of pepper might well have prevented such a shameful destruction of public property!" Applause and desk-thumping from his side as he sat down.

Back where we were sitting and down the bench from me the Red-haired Guy said. "Yes! Finally. Some common sense!"

"What's his problem?" I said to the Geezer.

"He's doing it for that microphone," he said, and pointed to the corner of a rafter above him where, sure enough, there was a mic. "That's to pick up what the visitors are saying," said the Geezer. "His job is to sit under it, so that when people hear the broadcast they hear what they think is public opinion, but is really only just him, paid to agree with the Government."

So he wasn't insane. It was politics. And not just like one of Grady's lies, either, improvised on the spot and mostly to save face, but a carefully planned strategy of lying which had been discussed, organized, rehearsed...

And I got that red raging in my head, that feeling that's the opposite of an idea for a poem. Oh, come off it, I thought, and then, like a bubble of gas, the thought swelled up and popped out of me.

"Oh, come *off* it!" I said, out loud.

And I didn't think I was shouting, but I got a loud voice, and as it happens, it fell into one of those sudden silences that sometimes occur in a room full of people, and it hung there for a second, clear and unmistakable, and on the floor there was some tittering and one big guffaw, then real laughter as the Red-haired Guy looked at me in shock, then, seeing people looking at him from the floor, he turned his back and made himself small as he gathered papers and backed out toward the hall.

A security guard tapped me on the shoulder.

"Excuse me," he said. "Could you please step this way?"

"Would you like me to help?" the Geezer asked me.

"Yeah," I said, and I cocked my thumb at the guard. "This guy wants to bounce me."

"Ma'am..." said the security guard.

And I hate that. "Don't "Ma'am" me," I said.

Then some other security guard came toward us, because obviously I've become a two-man problem. And I don't mind leaving, I mean, what's the big deal about Parliament, anyway? But the fact they want to kick me out for doing the same thing that the Red-Haired guy was doing, actually, just more honestly and out in the open, well, it makes me want to, like, chain myself to the bench and scream bloody murder.

"I'm with her," said the Geezer to the guard, and then to me. "This is idiotic, anyhow."

So they led both of us out to the hall and down to the coat-check where I picked up my bag and left, but there's still, like, smoke coming out of my ears, while the Geezer, who I guess didn't want to crowd me, stood back and started frittering with his little tablet computer, giving me a chance to cool down.

"You wouldn't perhaps know how these things work, do you?" he said after a while.

And he was being nice, I know, but I was still angry.

"Just because I'm young I'm supposed to understand computers?"

"No offence intended," he said, and he really looked appalled that he might have been impolite. "It's just, well, they've given me this new gadget..." and he exhaled one long frustrated sigh. "I mean, I covered the Canadian involvement in the Korean War, and the establishment of the De-Militarized Zone in South East Asia. I worked the Middle East bureau, covered the Six Day War and the Iranian Revolution. But these damn things," he shook the computer, "have completely defeated me. Are they any use at all?"

I was sorry I'd snapped at him. He was old and was gonna be dead soon anyhow, so I might as well be nice. "Naw, they're all garbage," I said. "You can borrow my pencil if you want."

"Ah," he said. "A pencil. Lovely," and he took it and handed me the computer.

"Want some paper?" I said.

"May I?"

"Sure," and I ripped out the centre page of my notebook and handed the whole notebook to him to have something to write on.

He smiled then looked over the top of his glasses and said, "Now you know why he didn't want to let you sit there."

"That's pathetic."

"It may be effective, though. Or at least they must think so."

I liked the way he talked. Dead clear, like Bertrand Russell's writing.

"What are you?" I said. "Some sort of reporter?"

"Retired. My nephew called me back to help out with his weblog."

"Well, why don't you write something about why they lie?"

"I do. But I'm supposed to be interviewing you. So. From what you've seen today, what's your overall impression?"

"Idiots."

"Who would you vote for?"

"I wouldn't."

"I mean, if you were forced at gunpoint, then who?"

"Well, duh, the guy who was asking the questions."

He made a note. "How do you spell "duh"?"

"You making fun of me?"

"I suppose so. But I would really like to know. Why wouldn't you vote for the Government?"

"If they're in charge, they're to blame."

"They're just human."

"So am I, but I'm not like that."

"Well, long may you preserve your innocence, my dear. Now. Could I have your name?"

And for a split second I thought, hey, I'm going to be famous! And then I thought that this is how Jimmy Fisher must've felt, so I said, "Marcia Watkins," which was the first name that sprang to mind, I guess because I'd just tried to phone her.

"Okay, Marcia," he said.

I handed him back his computer. "Here," I said. "You gotta hold down the switch until the logo comes onscreen." He took it back and looked at it light up.

"I see," he said. "Hunh."

"How do you spell 'hunh'?" I said.

He smiled again, a nice old-guy smile. "It was extremely pleasant to have met you, my dear," he said, and he gave me back my pencil and notebook and folded his piece of paper and put it in his pocket and held out his hand and I shook it. Then he said he had to go phone in his story, and there were almost no more phone-booths around since computers had taken over, and I told him that there was one in that hotel where I'd phoned Marcia's mom from. He started to leave, saying, "Bye, Marcia," which made me kind of sorry that I'd lied to him about that. But it's my life. Nobody said I *had* to want to be famous.

I walked back past the temporary-till-the-oil-supply-runs-out flame, and this time I stopped to read the signs of the protesters who wanted to halt the pipeline going through to the west coast, which of course was something I'd heard about, but had always thought, so what? Don't people have something better to think about? Like poetry?

Then I walked to where we'd parked the limo and where Grady was putting his guitar back in the trunk.

8

Heading North

It was a day and a half later before Grady let me
down again, but all that day and most of the next,
things were good between us.

We drove back to the Queensway and out of town
up the Ottawa Valley as the landscape changed from
suburbs to vacant land to farmland, through a band of
grey stone layer cake roadcuts and into countryside
where pines like giant bonsai trees grew on knuckles of
grey-pink granite, the first Canadian Shield on the trip
so far.

The landscape looked familiar because I'd seen
some of it in black and white pictures in Mom's photo
album from when she was researching her family. Her
great-grandmother's crowd had landed in Quebec City
from Britain and come up here in 1880 or something,
and her great grandfather and his wife had both died
from "galloping consumption," whatever that is. But

the twelve orphans they'd left were sent across the country by train, dropped off one by one with any relative who'd have them, in different towns, spreading them out so they wouldn't be too much of a burden on any one family. Some of us ended up in lumber towns in Northern Ontario, and some on Prairie farms, and Mom's grandmother had made it as far as the Kootenays. But the Ottawa Valley was their first home in the New World, free land if you could clear it, although it must've been a shock when they saw what they'd got, hills of solid rock between beaver ponds with dead trees standing out of the water.

Somewhere up by Prescott, Grady yawned. "Would you like to take over driving?" he said.

"I don't know how."

"Well, I'll teach you."

"It's illegal, Grady."

"It's a grey area."

"No it's not. It's black and white."

"Yeah, but Thea, black and white makes gray." Which should be, like, his motto.

"It's against the law, Grady."

"I'm just messing with you again, Thea," he said. "Here," and he reached into the slot in the door and took out a book and handed it across to me, The Official MTO Driver's Handbook.

I opened it and flipped through.

"I picked up a copy in Ottawa," said Grady. "You *should* know how to drive, and I figure that if you bone up on the rules, you can pass the exam on the road."

"At least in Ontario," I said.

"What?"

"It says here that you can only legally drive as a learner in the same province as you passed the test."

"Oh...Well, not to worry. We still got a whole lot of Ontario to drive through yet. I'll phone ahead to Sault St Marie for an appointment."

"Where you gonna phone from?"

"Actually when I say I *should*, I mean to say I already have. When I was in Ottawa."

"So why lie about it?"

"Sorry...But, hey Thea! This'll be fun!"

"Maybe."

But I thought that it was nice of him to do all that for me, and I felt bad about doubting the reasons he'd offered to teach me after Matnagut, so all the way up to the sandy country around Petawawa and beyond I studied the MTO Driver's handbook, and I got it pretty well down by the time we reached Mattawa, where I looked up and saw the river narrower between steep hills.

Grady stopped at a light then turned off toward North Bay.

"That was an illegal manoeuver," I said. "You changed lanes when you were turning."

He sighed dramatically. "Oh God," he said. "What have I wrought?"

◆—╫◆╫—◆

We slept outside North Bay that night and went on the next day in the rain to Sault St. Marie, stopping at the strip mall where Grady had made the appointment for my driving test. I got everything together I needed and memorized our license plate number and then went in, right on time.

Half an hour later I came out again.

"Want me to drive?" I said.

"You passed!"

"Easy-peasy."

"Good for you, Thea." He was proud, and so was I. I guess it was like "The Celebrities." Even though it was stupid, you still like to pass The Test.

"It's probably better if I'm the one who drives us through town," said Grady. "But after that we'll find a stretch where you can practice."

"Okay."

I was feeling good.

Then we passed a billboard outside an arena announcing that Chuck T. Boggs was playing there that night, and Grady said, "Hunh! I should go check this out."

And it all seemed a bit convenient.

"What for?" I said

"Might get some more work out of him. Or at least a hotel room. I could do with a shower."

"Why would he give you a hotel room?"

"What? Oh. Well...You never know."

"And how are you gonna know which hotel he's staying at?"

"Chuck T? It'll be the most expensive one."

And sure enough, at the first hotel Grady went to, there was Chuck T's bus.

We parked and Grady got out. "I'll go see if there's a chance," he said. "No use both of us going in."

So I stayed and wrote a haiku. It was vicious and hateful, and after I wrote it I tore it out of my notebook and crumpled it into a ball and burnt it in the ashtray and spat on the ashes.

A few minutes later Grady came back. "We're in luck. Somebody dropped out from the tour and we can take his room."

Which couldn't be right because wouldn't they just get the money back from any room they weren't using?

So I asked him, "Why did you bring your guitar with you?"

"What?"

"In Ottawa. What did you need the guitar for when you went to pick up the cheque?" It seemed connected.

"What? Oh...that...well... the E string was buzzing on a fret, and I wanted a guy at a music shop I know to take a look at it..."

I sighed to myself. "And did you?"

"Did I what?"

"Get it fixed."

"What? Oh yeah. Sure." Then he changed the subject. "Anyhow, I guess I should go see his concert, on account of him giving us the room, and maybe I'll meet up with him after, to talk to him about any other gigs."

I got out and followed Grady past three guys with elaborately coiffed facial hair standing outside the bus, smoking and looking bitter. On the side of the bus was a giant painting of Chuck T with the most elaborately coiffed beard of all.

"He looks like a Yahoo," I said.

"Pulls in a good-sized crowd though."

"And what's with the beard?"

"Maybe that helps bring 'em in."

"Anything but the songs, eh?"

"They're not bad, though he doesn't write 'em himself. Got a team in Nashville to crank out his hits."

"Why don't you do that?"

"Get other people to write my songs? Where's the fun in that?"

Grady had already checked in, so we went to the room and he threw his guitar case and bag onto the bed and went into the bathroom to shave. When I heard the water running, I opened the case and took out the guitar. It was worn and scratched with pearly dots up the neck.

"Whatcha doing, Thea?"

He was standing there with his face all lathered up.

"I've always wanted to learn how to play."

"Really?"

"Yeah."

"Well, I'll give you the first lesson while I'm shaving."

"OK."

He stepped back into the bathroom and I heard his voice, "First, just give it a strum. Run your right hand over the strings. Go ahead."

I did, and it sounded okay. "It needs cleaning," I said.

"The guitar? Never! It destroys the animal spirits."

I looked at it up close. "Which fret was buzzing?"

"What?" he said with a strange voice caused by pulling his face out of shape to shave.

"You said that the fret was buzzing and you had to get it fixed."

"Oh. Yeah. Um, twelfth, I think. Somewhere up there, anyway. Now, strum again."

I strummed to make him think I was doing what he told me while I counted up the neck and looked closely. All the frets around the twelfth were just as dirty and gummed up as the others. Nothing had been touched.

Grady came out of the bathroom, bald-faced: "We'll make a country music star of you yet," he said, and I put the guitar down.

I washed up as he dressed to go to Chuck T's concert, and we both left the room together, him to the arena and me to the limo, thinking that maybe he was going to be the opening act again, though he hadn't taken his guitar with him, so that couldn't be it... Unless he borrowed another one...

Also, that sob story about Art Cheadle didn't really apply to him, because Grady didn't have children who wanted him locked up or a wife who'd run away with his priest. Grady had gone on his three-year bender for some other reason, probably because it was beginning to look like he was never going to be a "star," and if that was the case, well, boo hoo, welcome to the rest of the human race.

Next morning I met him in the lobby for breakfast. "Thea!" he said. "Something's come up."

And I thought, oh boy, here it comes. "What?"

"I'm taking somebody to the airport first, and you're not allowed to drive if there's somebody else in the car, or so you were saying." Making it sound like I'd have to be okay with something I'd told him.

"Who?"

"Chuck T Boggs."

"What's wrong with his bus?"

"Jeez, Thea. You can't expect a superstar like him to be driving with his band!" Like a joke. "I met him again last night, see? After his concert?"

"Un-hunh."

"Half-decent concert, incidentally. For what it was, I mean. The band knew what they were doing, and the songs were a bit *processed*, but everybody got what they expected, which is something, I suppose..."

"Grady..."

"Sorry. So, afterwards we were hanging around his room and he mentions that he needed to get to the airport next day, so I figure why not?"

"Okay."

"So, what I suggest we do is this. We wait for Chuck T Boggs, drive him to the airport, then we continue on our merry way, with you driving. What do you say?"

"What am I supposed to say? You've already made up your mind."

"Thanks Thea. I'll make it up to you."

When the guy behind the desk wasn't looking I took a bunch of bagels and cheese and oranges from the breakfast table and snuck them out to the limo where I put them in my cabinet under the books. It was a "complimentary" breakfast so it wasn't really theft but frankly, I didn't care whether it was or not.

I got back to the lobby and there, like a walking advertisement for the International Yahoo Movement, was Chuck T. Boggs. He was wearing a fur coat and a Stetson, cowboy boots and of course sunglasses, because although there are posters of Chuck T Boggs all over the lobby, and the local paper's got Chuck T Boggs on the front page, and outside the hotel there's a bus with an eight-foot painting of Chuck T Boggs on the side, he was safe from being recognized, because he was wearing sunglasses.

He was standing over by the breakfast table, practicing looking fed up with his fans. The TV in the corner was playing footage of a burning cop car.

Grady came back in, nods at Chuck T and then saw the TV.

"Hey!" he said. "We were just there!" It was the native protest at Matnagut.

"Goddamn Indians," said Chuck T.

I mean, he actually *said* that. Then he walked to the centre of the lobby and took off his sunglasses so people can say, 'It's him! It's really him!' and nobody did, so he took two steps toward me and held out his hand.

I look at it but don't do anything so he grabbed *my* hand, shook it and said, "Chuck T Boggs. Pleased to meet ya."

"I'll never wash this hand again," I said.

But he doesn't get it, just looks me up and down, perving a little bit, which is disgusting because he's like forty years old if he's a day.

"I like your boots (henh henh)," he said.

And oh! The wit! Because he *doesn't* like them, see? So instead he says that he *does* like them, and you can tell that it's humour because he said "henh henh" afterwards, which gives him his own laugh-track, and that's handy because it's not likely anybody would ever find anything he said laughable.

I hated him. I hated not knowing what he had to do with us, and I was sick of waiting for an answer.

But then Grady gave a little laugh himself. "Yeah. Well, Thea's got a mind of her own," he said.

And why was he on Chuck T's side?

Chuck T glanced down at the luggage and gestured with his head.

"Oh Yeah?" said Grady. "You want service, do you?" and pretending to me like he's putting on an act of being a servant, he rolled his eyes. Chuck T turned, wobbled and made for the door with a little stumble and quick recovery. It's eleven o'clock in the morning and he was stoned or drunk or both. I followed them outside to the limo, and I got in the front seat as Chuck T climbed in the back.

"Turn on the radio," he said.

"Don't have one, Chuck T. It was ripped off."

"Get that fixed," he said. So he either didn't have a clue where he was, or what was becoming increasingly more obvious, Grady was back to telling lies, or actually, never stopped.

We passed a group of native protesters holding signs, and Chuck T said, "Shouldn't be allowed."

I'd had enough. "What shouldn't?" I said.

"Protesting" he said. "People shouldn't protest," like he was reciting one of the fundamental axioms of all Yahoos.

"But if you're saying that they shouldn't," I said, "well, that's a protest."

"So?"

"So if you say people shouldn't be allowed to protest, then you shouldn't be allowed to protest either."

Behind me it was like the gears in his head ground into place. "Yeah?" he said, and you could almost hear something click. "Well... I'm not people."

And I was thinking, you're right about that, Chuck T. Not likely anyone will ever mistake you for a human.

Then we got to the airport and Grady pulled up to Departures, and Chuck T started to get out, and Grady didn't exactly leap out of the driver's seat and run around to open the door for him, but it was close.

As Grady came around the front I powered down the window a crack so they wouldn't know I could hear them.

Chuck T Boggs said, "See you in Thunder Bay."

"Okay," said Grady. "Stay warm." Then he ran back around and got in. "Next stop, Thunder Bay."

"We can probably go further tonight, Grady."

"Yeah but...I'll be getting tired driving by then."

"I can drive."

"Um, yeah, I guess you can now. But no. I'd like to stop there if it's all the same to you. There's a place I want to show you that might still have some fall colours... Also, I'd like to talk to somebody there."

"Oh? Who?"

"It's just some business."

"You mean like Matt at the theatre in Moncton?"

"Now, Thea, I explained that to you..."

"No you didn't. You just made up another story to explain it, which was also a lie."

"Don't be like that, Thea. Just enjoy the scenery."

"Oh boy! Another tree! Well, that's different! Oh look! "Another one..."

"Okay, Thea..."

I looked right at him. "I heard Chuck T Boggs say he'd see you in Thunder Bay."

He paused. "Yeah, well... that's who I gotta meet." Like he was glad that was all cleared up now.

We pulled out of the airport and drove to a stop sign before the Trans Canada.

"You owe Chuck T Boggs money, don't you, Grady?"

He glanced at me surprised, then, realizing he might be giving it away, his eyes snapped up and started to perform this, like, elaborate dance of evasion. They shot over to check out some possible danger on the other side of the road, then back to the stop sign and finally they blinked twice and settled into a straight-ahead look under steady lids. "Sorry. What?" he said.

"You heard me."

"I...I'm sorry," he said, like he had been occupied with a minor driving problem which had just been taken care of, and now I had his full attention. "What did you say?"

"I said that you heard me."

"Heard you what?"

"Heard me say that you owe Chuck T Boggs some money."

He paused. "Ah."

"Which explains what we're doing."

"Well, no... Not in the way you're thinking..."

"How do you know how I'm thinking?"

"I don't. That's not what I'm saying. But... Oh, what's the difference? We're here aren't we? It's a beautiful day. You don't have to occupy yourself with any of those things."

"I shouldn't worry my pretty little head about it?"

"Not like that. But..." Then he said something that really ticked me off. "Here Thea, I know! Why don't you take over at the wheel?"

I loathed him.

"Okay," I said.

"Okay?" he said, a bit surprised. "All right!" and he pulled over and I got out and walked around to the driver's side and got in.

"Right!" he said. "Now. That's your brake, and that's your gas. Anything goes wrong, just hit the brake. First though, check if the mirrors are alright."

He showed me how to adjust them, and when I could see around me he said, "Comfy?"

"No."

"Well, you'll get used to it. The main thing is to watch that you don't ram into anybody or let anybody ram into you."

"Supposing they do."

"Well, that means we're all dead. But don't worry about it. You're smart, Thea. No need to be nervous."

But I wasn't nervous. Just angry. Seething.

"Okay now," said Grady. "Seat belt attached. Look both ways, turn around and look into your blind spot."

"If it's a blind spot how can I look into it?"

"It's just what they call it, what the mirrors don't cover. Turn your head and look if there's anybody there. Is there?"

"No."

"Okay. Now, put it into drive and step on the gas slowly..."

I did like he said and the car started to roll forward.

"Okay," he said. "Good...Now, pull out onto the road and push down on the gas some more... now pick up speed... You're doing great, Thea. Just stay in this lane, and keep it between the ditches, like Barry Cameron used to tell me. He was the guy who taught me how to drive. 'Keep her out of the rhubarb, Grady,' he'd say. 'Between the ditches, rubber side down'..."

"Grady!"

"What?"

"I'm trying to drive!"

"Doin' good, Thea. Don't have to be so tense, though." He looked behind. "Okay. Now. Here comes a truck..."

"What do I do?"

"Take it easy. He's miles away... coming fast though. But don't worry."

I looked in the rearview mirror and saw the truck way down the highway, a big angry grill barreling toward us, getting bigger. He'd ram into us and plow us off the side of the road and we'd flip and explode into flames and we'd all be dead. At least I wouldn't be on this stupid trip with a bunch of Yahoos like Chuck T Boggs and Grady.

"You might want to keep it in the right lane though..." said Grady.

I'd wandered over, so I yanked the wheel to get back.

"Easy now, just sort of ease it back. You can do this."

I looked in the side mirror and the truck had halved the distance between us.

"He's going to pass, Thea, but don't worry. Get back in the right lane again, though..."

The truck came up fast until it was looming in the rear view mirror, and the jerk who was driving hit his horn, a real long angry blast.

It was typical. These idiots with their big toys ramming through wherever they want, like Chuck T, like Grady.

So when he goes to pass, I move over and wouldn't let him. He honks his horn again, and until then I didn't even know where the horn was, but I'd seen them do it on TV, so I hammer my fist on the middle of the wheel and made not much of a sound compared to his, but more annoying, so that was satisfying.

But he honks again, Toot! Toot! so I honk back in the same rhythm, sarcastically, and then I see him trying to pass on my right. I mean, I've only been driving for two minutes and I know that's illegal. So, fine, I think, you want to play, I'll play too.

He noses up behind me on my right, and we're both doing one-twenty now and he honks again and I look in the side mirror and see his big ugly bulldog face, and then he actually flips me the finger, which is like, *rude*, so I flip one back and speed up so he can't pass. And he honks again, so, so do I. And the spruce trees are snapping past now, and there's a sign that says one-ten, but we're doing one-forty, and I hear this strangled unnnh! sound and I glance over and Grady is pointing one weak finger straight out front.

So I look, and way ahead I see another truck coming toward us over the hill in the lane I'm halfway in now.

But he's just going to have to pull over and out of my way, because no way am I backing down.

And I guess Jerkface in the truck beside me is thinking the same, because he isn't slowing down, either, just keeping pace at one-forty now, and now the guy coming toward us starts honking, long frightened please-God-what's-happening horn sounds, and the limo is starting to shake with the speed which is up to one-sixty. And Grady is staring and praying, Oh God Oh God Oh God. And the guy in the truck coming down the hill towards us brakes and fishtails as he pulls off to his side of the road as I pass him and Jerkface beside me drops back too, because it's too rich for his blood, the chicken... and just as I'm thinking Yes! I've won! pulling away from them both, feeling great and honking a few more times to celebrate my victory, I bounce over the brink of that hill and that's when I see right in front of me, the moose.

Striding out of a swamp, young and totally clueless. So I lean on the horn, slam on the brakes and screech to a long halt.

The moose turns, hops and strides away into the woods.

Everything is suddenly very quiet, like Time has stopped, like we're both dead and this is the afterlife.

Then Time started again, and I looked over at Grady.

His eyes were staring out of a white mask, fixed
directly at the dashboard where there was nothing to see,
"Pull Over To The Side Of The Road," he said, dead calm,
pronouncing each word clearly. "Take Your Foot Off The
Brake And *Don't* Put Your Foot On The Gas."

I did. The car rolled forward to the shoulder.

"Now Put Your Foot On The Brake. Now. Put The
Gearshift Into Park. And Turn Off The Engine."

I did.

He exhaled.

"Well?" I said. "What's going on?"

He looked directly at me. "What is 'going on', Thea,
is that you nearly killed us both."

"Well you deserve to be killed if you keep lying to me."

"I 'deserve to be killed'?"

"Yes! If you don't tell me what's going on."

He sighed, blinked, sighed again and said, "I am
trying to earn a living. Okay? Is that all right with you?
Does that meet your oh-so-high moral standards?"

"No. It doesn't. And no, it's not all right. It's all wrong."

I heard a noise behind us and Jerkface in the truck
roared past us honking into the distance ahead. Through
his back window I could see him bouncing up and down
in his seat, gesturing like an idiot and flipping me the
finger some more.

I said, "The guitar, Grady."

"What about it?"

"In Ottawa. You said you got it fixed. But you never
did."

He paused, thought, then looked at me directly.
"Yeah? Well, *you* lied to me."

"I *lied* to *you?*"

"When you pretended you didn't know it hadn't been fixed."

"Yeah! Because *you* lied to *me* about getting it fixed, and if I'd asked you straight you woulda lied to me again. I wanted to find out the truth."

"By lying?"

"Look Grady, don't you dare try and turn this around. Why did you bring the guitar with you in Ottawa?"

"Because I needed it to play on the street, okay? For some money. So we wouldn't starve."

"Beaumont didn't pay you in Ottawa either?"

"Well, sort of. They gave me a credit card for gas."

"*You* said..."

"Yes! I know. But they were only going to pay for the gas, so I brought the guitar with me to play on the street for *food*. So we could eat! Jeez!"

"Ok, then." I put the key into the ignition and started the limo.

He grabbed hold of my hand tight. "What do you think you are doing?" he said.

"I'm driving."

"I am never, *ever*, going to let you drive again."

"I *like* driving!"

"I don't care."

"Look, Grady..."

"No!"

"Why not?"

"Because I said so."

"That's not a reason."

And he looked at me, and took the key out of the ignition and said, "It's reason enough for you, young lady. I Am Your Father."

He opened the door and stepped out and walked around the front. I got out and walked around the back. Outside a few flakes of snow were falling out of a grey sky, and I shivered. But part of me liked him telling me that.

I mean, what do you gotta do?

9

We Lose Our Minds

If Lake Superior looks like the head of a wolf, that day we drove from the back of its neck across the top of its head to the bridge of its nose at Thunder Bay, up and over long spruce hills with sudden views of the lake so big you could never see the far shore. We got ahead of the weather and by afternoon we were driving on dry clean highway in the sun.

Grady was giving *me* the silent treatment now, but just before the hotel outside Thunder Bay where we were supposed to pick up Chuck T, he finally spoke up.

"I didn't win that card game," he said.

"What a surprise."

"I lost it."

"Yeah well that's what 'not winning' usually means."

"Okay. But if you want to know the truth..."

"Why would I? Who cares?"

"The *truth*, Thea, is that I'm working off what I owe Chuck T by driving Beaumont's limo to Prince Rupert. OK? And I figured if nothing else I'd get to ride with you across country, and get you home at the same time as paying off what I owe him."

"Well, if you think I'm going to be sharing the rest of my ride with that pig!"

He sighed mightily. "You won't have to. He wants to make a big splashy entrance back at his hometown to show everybody how big a star he is, and after that I'm supposed to get him to the next airport to send him off, and then we can drive the rest of the way without him to Prince Rupert, where I leave it once and for all. Happy now?"

"No. Why would you hire on again with those jerks?

"Because I needed them to get you home."

"Oh *I* see. You were doing it for *me*."

"Yes, in fact."

"But Grady, only because you lost my airfare in the poker game!"

"OK."

"So, *why?*"

"Also...I wanted to get even with Chuck T, okay?"

"For what?"

"He stole my band, and got me kicked out of Beaumont's agency."

"How?"

"Some greasy little backroom deal...I never found out.... and I was in no shape then to fight for anything..."

"Why not?"

"I was... drinking."

"Oh great! You're a drunk, too."

"No."

"Ha!"

"I'm not. I could always take booze or leave it."

"For three years you couldn't."

"That's over."

"So you say."

"And so it is."

"How does it work, exactly?" I said. You put the bottle to your lips and like magic you can forget that you have, like, a *family?*"

"It's a bit more complicated than *that,* Thea."

"How? Seems perfectly straightforward to me. Family here. Bottle there. I'll take the booze please!" I felt tears welling up in my eyes, but I wasn't going to cry. "I mean, here I was thinking I was being driven across the country in his very own limo by my small-time dipstick country singer embarrassment of a father, but then, not only do I find out that the limo *isn't* his, but that he's not *even* a small-time dipstick country singer embarrassment, but rather the limo driver for another even-more-of-a-dip-stick country singer embarrassment."

"Okay, Thea..."

"Why didn't you just tell me?"

"I guess I didn't want my daughter to think I was a small-time country singer embarrassment."

"Dipstick."

"What?"

"I didn't say you were a small-time country singer embarrassment, Grady. I said you were a small-time *dipstick* country singer embarrassment. Of a father. Who, after a three-year bender, wants to make me feel sorry for *him* about it."

"Okay..."

"I mean, the way I see it, you're on stage, you're making money, and you know, Grady, most people at the end of their rigorous two-hour workday don't have a roomful of people applaud them. So you got it pretty easy compared to a lot of people, and you could be, like, grateful. But instead you think, 'I must really *be* something'. And although you have never seen or heard of anybody who has successfully managed their life while drinking twenty-four hours a day, you are feeling so incredibly special that you think, 'I could be the first'."

I waited for Grady's answer.

But then we arrived at the hotel where we were supposed to pick up Chuck T.

—‖••‖—

"Hi Marcia."

"Thea! How are you?"

"Good."

"Where are you?"

"Thunder Bay."

I was phoning her from the lobby of the hotel.

"I'm still in Prince Rupert," said Marcia. "But I'm getting ready to leave for Pritchit to help out Daisy."

"I'm gonna be in Pritchit myself in a few days."

"No way!"

"Yep."

"Cool!"

"Yeah."

I was glad to hear her voice. It cheered me up.

"*And*," she said, "I was talking to Mom and I found something for Grady."

"Really?"

"It's a November Eleventh thing. Honouring the war dead, you know."

"Great! How'd you get it?"

"Daisy's trying to expand her demographic, according to Leland..."

"Who?"

"Daisy's manager. And Leland asked Daisy, and apparently (I can't believe it) Daisy actually *knows* Grady."

"Yeah, that's what Grady said."

"And apparently he's got a song, 'Soldier Home,' which would be perfect for the occasion."

"Really?"

"Yeah. So, anyway, you're in."

"Well... thanks Marcia."

"No problem..." and she gave me all the necessary info about the booking, and we told each other what we'd been up to, how she thought it didn't look like Daisy's protest was going to be as big as they thought it would be with all the other protests happening now after Matnagut, and I said that I'd been there, and she said No way! and then we gabbed about this-and-that, though not the House of Commons, because I wanted to save that for when I saw her face to face, and finally we said goodbye and hung up.

I walked out of the hotel and got in the back of the limo. Grady poked his head in, but before I could tell him about the gig, he said, "Better ride in the front with me, Thea."

"I like it here."

"Ah Thea, don't make this any more difficult than it has to be."

"Well I don't see why..." I start to say, but then there's a noise, the door of the hotel bangs open and Chuck T comes out making a bee-line for the open limo door. Grady says "Ok Ok Ok" and gets out of the way just as Chuck T falls past him through the limo door onto the floor inside and I have to move my feet out of the way while he rolls onto his knees, and crawls into his seat where he sits facing me. Behind him on the other side of the partition I see Grady slide into the driver seat, start the limo and pull away. Apparently we're in a hurry.

Chuck T closes his eyes, opens them again, belches, then notices there's somebody else with him. He gives me a long pervy gander, like it's his right. Then he drifts off again, burps, drools, and nods off to sleep, but even then he manages to act like a jerk. He snores like a bear, then farts so I have to open the window. I mean, it takes real talent to be both unconscious *and* obnoxious at the same time. We're driving out into the country under a beautiful sky, darker blue than summer, with that late fall sun that I love, but I can't enjoy it because of this big smelly lump in my space. And it gets worse. Five minutes later he wakes up and his first words are, "You got any liquor?"

"No."

"Why not? You got a liquor cabinet," and he looks at it.

"It's for my books."

"Why? Can't drink books." And he laughs like he's cracked a real good one. He digs around in his pockets and takes out a pillbox and pops a pill. "I only do 'em to keep my weight down," he says, and I think, Better take a few more then, you fat pig. "And that's my last one," he says. "What can you do if you got no drink or drugs?" And he looks at me. "How about some sex?"

Well, what a surprise, I thought.

"So?" he says. "Wanta do it?" Apparently he's serious.

"No."

"C'mon. We could do it right here."

"Not if I kick you in the testicles."

And he acts mock-shocked. "A saucy one, are you?" and he pats the seat beside him. "Come on over here and let's have a taste of some of that sauce."

"I have AIDS," I say

His face drops. "Really?"

"No, you moron. But I don't want to have sex with you, okay? Even if you weren't really old, and really *really* ugly, which you really really are, I still wouldn't like your stupid clothes, your stupid attitude, and your stupid beard. I still wouldn't like *you*."

But people don't say things like that to the great Chuck T Boggs. He turns in his seat and says loudly to Grady. "Get her out of here."

"What's happening?" says Grady.

"He wants to have sex with me, Father," I say.

"'Father'?" says Chuck T.

Grady pulls off to the side of the highway and hops out, angry about having to deal with all this, and he closes the door hard. Chuck T thinks the anger is towards him and he hustles out the other side of the limo to face Grady coming around the front.

I follow Chuck T out, as Grady, getting near, starts slowing down wondering whether he is supposed to fight or not. Though I wouldn't mind seeing him take a swing at Chuck T, whose backing away, making calm-down gestures with his hands. And he backs into me, so I kick him in the back of the ankle and he yells and turns, steps on to soft gravel and stumbles off the shoulder of the highway, then lurches back to stop himself from falling by grabbing for my arm.

But I swing it out of his way, and he hits me in the tits. And okay, he didn't mean it, but it still hurt. So I gasp and wind up and slap him in the face real hard and he says "Bitch!" and Grady says "Hey!"

But now I'm next to the open back door of the limo so I duck back into the backseat, then look back to see Chuck T, not after me, necessarily, maybe just trying to get away from Grady, but grabbing my ankle to pull himself in and I twist around onto my back to kick him away with my other foot as Grady grabs the back of his jacket and pulls. And I see Chuck T drag back then break free and his face suddenly gets big in the door as he makes a lurch to get inside, and you could hear his forehead go clunk! on the door frame and his grip on my ankle goes slack and I reach for the far door handle and scramble back out of the other side of the limo and look across the roof to see Chuck T standing up straight

holding his forehead and swaying. And you shouldn't
straighten up suddenly after hitting your head, particularly when you're old like him. The blood rushes out of
his tiny brain and he collapses onto the ground out of my
sight. And I run around back to see he's lying there
completely quiet.

"Oh Jesus," says Grady. "Oh Jesus Jesus Jesus. What
do we do now?"

"Leave him."

"We can't just beat him up and leave."

"He beat himself up."

"Still, Thea..."

But I could still feel his grip on my ankle. No way
could I have broken free. "But first," I said, "we'll shave
him."

"No, Thea. I don't think we ..."

"I'm doing it." And I reached in my bag for my folding
scissors which I took out and opened up. I crouched
down, grabbed a fistful of beard and snipped it off his
face.

"Thea...Don't..."

"He was trying to rape me, Grady."

Which may not have been one hundred percent true.
More likely he didn't have a clue what he was doing, but
he'd frightened me. My heart was still thumping.

"Well, you don't know that he..."

"Don't apologize for him, Grady."

"Look, Thea..."

"I told him no, and he still came on to me."

"Yeah. Well...Are you okay incidentally?"

"Oh fine, thanks for finally asking!"

"I'm sorry. Look..."

"We're going to shave him, leave him, then we are going to get into the car and drive to Pritchit where I negotiated a show for you with Daisy Ratzinger. And from there we will continue to Prince Rupert so I can take the ferry to Haida Gwaii, like you told me we would." I pinched another good-sized lock of Chuck T's beard and snipped it off.

"You got me a gig?" said Grady.

"You're welcome," I said, and as I grabbed Chuck T's beard and snipped it lock by lock I told him about my phone call to Marcia.

And these stage people, it must be like an addiction or something, because Grady watched me snip a few more times, then decided.

"Only do half," he said.

"What?"

"You don't have to shave his whole face. Shave just half and he'll have to shave the rest himself. Here. Let me help."

"Get your own scissors."

"I will." And he popped the trunk and brought back a pair, as well as a razor.

"I'll start on his eyebrows," he said.

"Good idea."

Grady shaved one eyebrow, then leant back, looked at it and said, "That's for stealing my band." And he grabbed a lock of head hair and snipped it with his scissors. (Snip) "And that's for plotting with Beaumont to get me kicked out!" (Snip SNIP). And that's for waiting for the (Snip) right moment, (Snip) when I was in no shape to fight back, right after I heard..."(SNIP SNIP SNIP SNIP *SNIP*) "And that's for being a piece of crap sell-out third-rate cut-throat no-talent arse-kissing...You bastard!" he said, breathing hard, then stopped talking and just kept snipping.

"Watch you don't cut his ear," I said.

"Yeah. That'd be a real tragedy," he said. They say revenge is sweet, but this looked as bitter as bile."

"OK, Grady. That's enough..."

"It's *not* enough. He tried to rape my daughter!"

"Well..."

He looked at me. "What?"

"I don't know if he actually was trying to, like, exactly..."

"What are you saying?"

It was like if we allowed ourselves to think he hadn't tried to rape me then we'd be the bad guys. Wanting to be on the side of Good, we were wishing for a bad thing to be true. Everything was upside down.

"He would have, though," I said. "If you hadn'ta been there."

"Goddamn right!" said Grady and he swelled up again. "And the bastard had it coming to him anyway! I mean, he coulda got anybody to drive his goddamned limo but he wanted to rub my face in it and show the rest of his band who was boss." He crouched down again. "Don't look so big now, do you 'boss'?"

He dug into Chuck T's back pocket and took out his wallet and opened it. "Thirty bucks!" he said. "Cheap bastard," and he took the money and dropped the wallet onto the ground.

Chuck T blinked his eyes open and said "Gurk-urk..."

We hustled back into the limo and Grady started up and drove off and we didn't say anything for a few kilometres when we passed the exit to Chuck T's home-town where a big sign said "Welcome back Chuck T Boggs!" and we both burst out laughing.

And once we stopped Grady said, "Sorry, Thea. I didn't think you had to know."

"You didn't think, period."

"Okay. But the only reason I told you these stories ..."

"Lies."

"Lies, then, is because I didn't want my daughter to think I was, well, a ... loser."

"Well you are one, Grady." But the way I said it made it okay, like I didn't care one way or the other about that, which I don't, because, well, first last, last first, you know?

"I suppose I am," said Grady, not too broken up about it, either, so that was alright. "And hell, we're on our way to a gig, aren't we?"

"Yeah!"

"Driving a big limo, too!"

But then we passed a Native souvenir shop with a cop car in the parking lot and I knew what Grady was thinking, because I was thinking the same thing.

"Chuck T may not report us," I said.

"Why not?"

"Well, for one thing he'd have to admit he got beat up by a girl."

Grady thought a bit. "You could be right..."

"And he deserved it," I said, trying to get clear in my mind how that was, exactly. "And anyway, apart from everything else, he's a racist pig."

"Yeah, he is. That's true. But..."

"What?"

"When he was in my band, he had a bunch of Indian jokes he used to tell the audience, until we finally had to tell him to shut up. And then somebody told me that Chuck T's mother was Cree."

"Chuck T is native?"

"Half. Yeah. At least that's what his manager told me. So the way he acts might have something to do with... I don't know, *you* figure it out."

Which made everything more complicated, though it shouldn't have. I mean, there was no logical reason why it should. And I started to work out the steps that justified why it shouldn't, so that he would still be the bad guy, to justify what we'd done to him.

But at the same time I felt something move from my heart to my head, where I kept my mind away from that confusing wash of grey and into those safe and neat categories of black and white. Driving an angel from my door.

10

Fugitives from Justice

We drove to the other side of Kenora where we slept until Grady woke me and said it might be better if we travelled by night, so we headed for the Prairies under a moon so full you could see the landscape almost as clear as day. There were fewer trees and less rock here, and when we came onto flat land we passed through smoke rolling off a prairie fire, a necklace of flame circling twenty acres of burnt land like black velvet.

Before Winnipeg we left the Trans Canada, thinking there wouldn't be as many cops on the back roads, and the landscape was different again now, with shallow lakes and sloughs like big wet fields, gleaming under that moon. And then I fell asleep for a while and when I woke we had crossed into Saskatchewan, bald prairie and thin rivers in gullies you came down into

and crossed over, then up the far bank onto the high
prairie again.

There weren't many gas stations here, though, and
when we finally found one Grady tried to pre-pay with
his credit card, but it had been cancelled, so he used the
cash he'd taken from Chuck T, and when he went to fill
up I hung around inside the station because we needed a
new map.

I went over to the rack, saw the one I needed, picked
up two, looked at them both and put only one back while
sliding the other into my handbag. Then I took a free
handout to have something for cover, thinking I was
getting *good* at this. But on the way to the cash I had
second thoughts.

This wasn't like the sugar cubes which I'd forgotten
I'd had in my purse, or the bible which I'd sort of surprised myself into stealing and didn't really know what I
was doing until it was done. I knew exactly what I was
doing here, and when you know you're doing something
wrong it's a whole lot harder to pull it off. So to calm
myself down I said to myself, okay, well I'm not out of
the store now, it's not a crime till I'm out of the store.
Then I went and put the handout on the counter and
tried to act like it was the only thing I'd taken.

The bored-stiff cashier was sitting with one knee up
watching TV, and he glanced at the handout and said
"It's free," then looked back at the tube where, on the
local entertainment news some girl with way too much
makeup was saying that there had been rumoured
sightings of one of "billionaire recluse Gordon
Beaumont's trademark magenta limousines."

I froze.

The guy at the cash turned and looked outside at our limo, then back at me.

"What colour is magenta?" he said.

"Yellow," I told him.

"Oh," he said, and turned back to the TV.

Boys. They're almost too easy.

—:|—:|—

That night we got halfway across Saskatchewan, slept for a while, then started a few hours before dawn and crossed the Alberta border just as the sun was rising.

"We won't have nearly enough gas to get us to Pritchit," said Grady.

"Stop in the next town and play your guitar on the street."

"Around here they wouldn't know how to take it."

"How do you know till you've tried?"

"I grew up around here, Thea."

I'd forgotten. "So what are we going to do?"

Grady thought a bit, sucking his lip while driving. "Ah, to hell with it," he said, and he turned onto a concession road.

"Hey!" I said. "You're supposed to keep straight."

"Change of plan, Thea. Time to visit the family."

"Uncle Bernard?"

"How do you know about him?"

"Because I'm a poor discarded waif who longs to connect with her shattered family unit."

"Really?"

"Don't flatter yourself."

The concession road was paved for a hundred yards, then gravel for a kilometre or two where we came to another paved road and turned back east. We passed a sign for a bible camp, and a grain elevator in the distance took its own sweet time getting larger and larger the closer we came. Before we got to town a sign said "Homestead" and we took a feeder road to a willow grove where Grady rolled to a stop beside a slough with cattails and a duck box. There was a bent bike in a pile of junk and a rusting combine harvester like a mechanical dinosaur. In the willows sat a magpie nest, a mad pile of sticks.

"Old Man Brody's dump," said Grady. "This used to be our hiding place."

"It's the only cover as far as the eye can see. Think they might have guessed?"

Grady shrugged. "We were kids."

We walked back down the feeder road to a truck stop then into the town itself. Boarded up stores, a co-op, a dance studio, and a Chinese and Canadian restaurant. At the end of Main Street you could see bald prairie framed between the last two buildings.

Grady looked across the street at a church painted white, and another house next to it which must've been where the minister lived, because they'd painted and roofed it the same way. "He'll be around here somewhere," said Grady. "Bernard never strays too far from home. Or usen't to anyhow..." And sure enough, just as he said that the front door of the house opened and a distracted man in a dog-collar came out and walked toward the church. He looked familiar. Grady crossed to meet him and I followed.

Bernard, lost in his own thoughts with his lips moving and one hand making little gestures as he walked, didn't see us coming.

"Hi, Bernard," said Grady, and Bernard looked up with a jolt, snatched his breath back then blinked hard, twice.

"Grady?" he said, and he breathed out. "Is it you?"

"How you been?" said Grady.

"It's really you!" He looked around, then back. "But you couldn't have come at a worse time..."

Grady's face fell. "Well, if you want me to go, we'll just..."

"No no. It's good to see you. It really is. It's just... I mean, literally, you could not have... I'm sorry. We should talk."

"Sure," said Grady, then "This is Thea. Your niece."

"Thea... You're Thea?" said Bernard, and I nodded. "I heard about... But this is so strange. Well well..." He smiled broadly, then snapped back into worry.

"Look," he said. "I'm expecting some... people, but," he looked at his watch, "we have a few minutes before they're due. And yes, this is good. Could be a Godsend in fact. Here. Let's get into the church."

He led us to the front door but there was a chain wrapped through the handles with a large padlock. "Hmm," he said. "They must have.... Anyway. Let's try the vestry." And we walked around the side of the building where he took a key from a hiding place and opened the back door. "There was a time that no church in the country was ever locked," he said with a sigh. "But come in, please. Come in."

The vestry was cold and lined with dark wood and it smelled of mothballs and bee's wax. "Sit down. Please, sit," and he gestured to a pew over by the wall, which was as uncomfortable as any church pew I'd ever sat in. It's like, in case you were thinking of backsliding, they want to give you a taste of what Hell feels like.

Uncle Bernard took a seat behind his desk. On the wall behind him was a photograph of my grandfather, preaching, and I could see the family resemblance. I was glad I'd got my looks from Mom.

"So. How's your flock treating you, Bernard?" said Grady.

"Ready to revolt, actually."

"Really? Why?"

"Their money has disappeared."

"What happened to it?"

"They entrusted it to the church."

"Your church?"

"Yes."

Grady let this sink in. "We did come at a bad time."

"You have no idea," said Bernard.

"Where'd the money go?"

"It was stolen."

"By you?"

"Please, Grady..."

"Who then?"

"We don't know."

"How?"

Bernard slumped slightly and exhaled. "Oh Grady, they conned me," he said. "They played on my vanity and robbed me and my congregation blind."

"What happened?"

"A man came to town, parked his car out by Roy Hanson's quarter section, looked out over a field and made a note on his phone, then got back in and drove away. That's all.

"Perce Whitbourne saw it, told a few people, and two days later the same man came back and put a message on the co-op bulletin board and an ad in the paper saying that there would be a small explosion on Tuesday at the corner of that field where he'd stopped. So people were watching now. Tuesday came, he showed up, let off a small charge, looked at a computer and read off the results of the shock wave and Walt Meyers finally asked him what it was all about and the man said it was for an oil exploration team. 'Oil?' said Walt. 'Does this mean we're all going to be rich?' And the man said, 'It may very well mean just that.'"

"So word got around fast now."

"Walt told Pete Dougherty and Pete told me, and I invited the man, who claimed his name was Roger Dale, for tea. I asked him, naturally, how all this was likely to affect the community and he said that it would affect us greatly and that depended on... well, me."

"So I asked him how, and he said that he'd seen boomtowns before, and some were good and some were bad, but the bad ones all have one thing in common, and that is, no spiritual centre. He was playing me, I see that now. And I walked right into his trap, closed the door behind me and locked myself inside. 'Well, what do I do?' I said.

"And he whispered to me, 'Buy into it. There are going to be some big changes around here, and you are going to need some clout, and that means a stake in the business. If I were you, I would get as much money together and invest it all in as close to the source as possible.'

"'I'm sorry. I don't understand,' I said, and he had me. Within a week I was collecting money, absolutely convinced that we would be... not rich, it wasn't about the money, but I, *we*, would have a hand in things. Power." Bernard stopped.

"You didn't ask him why he would be giving you such a hot tip, I suppose," said Grady.

"He said he grew up as a street kid, and when he was sixteen and headed downhill fast, he'd met a man like me, a reverend in my denomination who turned him around and set him straight. He could never fully repay that man for his kindness, he said, but this was an attempt."

"So, what's this delegation you're waiting for?"

"A committee of concerned citizens who wish to address some issues they have with their spiritual leadership."

"You?"

"It has been rumoured that I am in the employ of the man who ripped us off."

"That would be bad."

"Yes."

"What are you gonna tell them?"

"I'll explain my position and see whether we cannot move beyond the immediate finger-pointing to a healthier plateau of self-awareness and forgiveness."

"Who's coming?"

"Grace Hopstaefl's sons."

"The Hopstaefl boys?"

"The same."

Grady thought for a second. "You're screwed," he said.

"No no. I'm sure I can reason with them."

"The Hopstaefls? Well...first time for everything, I suppose."

"You'll help me, won't you?"

"Um, Bernard, I'd like to... But you might need somebody afterwards to take you to the hospital."

"But..."

From outside the vestry we heard low muttering and the crunching of heavy boots on the gravel path. It got suddenly dark in the room as a group of large torsos passed in front of the window, like thunderheads in front of the sun.

"Here they are," said Bernard, and he pushed his glasses back up the bridge of his nose and straightened up in his chair, willing himself to be positive. "Come in!" he said, but they weren't asking permission. All four of them shouldered their way through the door and stepped to right in front of the desk where they clotted up in a group, scowling. The youngest was about nineteen and the oldest forty, the two in the middle were identical twins, and all of them were large and fit. When their eyes adjusted to the light they noticed me and Grady over by the wall, but judging I guess that we weren't a threat, they turned back and glowered at Bernard some more, all except the nineteen year old, who stood there with his mouth open, gazing directly at my tits. The eldest smacked him on the side of the head, and he blushed like an octopus and turned away.

Bernard coughed once. "Fergie, Farley, Fortner, Frank. Welcome welcome welcome. This is my brother and this is my niece."

Everybody nodded but didn't look back at us, except the youngest, Fergie, who threw a quick glance my way again.

I smiled back. Why not? He was kind of cute.

Frank, the oldest, put his fists on the desk, leant towards Bernard and looked him straight in the eye.

"So where's the money?" he said.

Bernard's face got incredibly sad and he looked back at Frank with big heavy eyes. "Gone," he said, then took a deep breath and sighed.

I thought of a way out of this, but right now might not be the best time to say anything.

"You said if we gave you our money we'd get more of it back," said Frank.

"I was deceived myself."

"Not as bad as us, though."

"Worse. The whole affair has caused a grievous breach of trust between myself and my congregation."

"Yeah but that's just your reputation. We lost our *money.*"

"They stole my money too, don't forget," said Bernard.

"You can always get more."

"How?"

"Move on to some other town with your pretty lies and your shiny shoes and lay some more traps for people like us. That's what people like you do. That's who you are. Dedicated dyed-in-the-wool con men, moving from town to town ripping off honest hard-working citizens."

"I've been here all my life."

"See what I mean? Dedicated."

"I..."

"There's nothing to say, Reverend. You took our money and now we're gonna take it back. From out of your hide."

"I'll give you everything I got," said Bernard.

"How much?"

"Sixty-five dollars?"

"Well, that's not four thousand dollars, now, is it?"

"All right, then we'll...I've got it! We'll... hold an auction! I'll make some posters and you can put them up at the Co-op..."

"Hear that, boys?" said Frank. "He wants us to do some more work for him."

The boys snorted with contempt.

"I think that we should all forgive us our trespasses as we forgive those who trespass against us," said Bernard.

"When have we ever trespassed against you?"

"Never, but...."

"Well, that doesn't apply, then, does it, Reverend?"

"Turn the other cheek?" said Bernard.

"An eye for an eye..." said Frank.

"'Vengeance is mine, sayeth the Lord'?"

"...And a tooth for a tooth." Frank lifted one of his fists off the desk. "Now. Any particular tooth you want me to knock out first?"

I looked at Grady but it was like his brain had locked, so whether it was the right time or not, I might have to say something soon.

"You would commit the sacrilege of an act of violence in the house of God?" said Bernard.

Frank stopped, looked around, then looked at his brothers, who all shrugged why not? "Seems as good a place as any," he said.

"But...I'm wearing glasses."

"Well, we'd best take them off, then." And Frank reached across and with both hands carefully took the glasses off Bernard's face then folded and placed them on the desk out of the way. The twins moved to either side and Frank grabbed Bernard by the collar.

I looked at Grady and he was still frozen, so I said, "Why don't you just beat up Gordon Beaumont himself?"

Frank stopped and looked around. "What?"

I stepped forward. "Gordon Beaumont." I was aware that I was bearing false witness against somebody I'd never even met, but this was no time for hairsplitting. "That was him who conned you," I said. "We know. He conned us too."

Frank squinted at me suspiciously. "How old are you?" he said.

"I know I look young, but I'm actually twenty three," and out of the corner of my eye I saw Fergie's face look suddenly disappointed. "Thea Jordan," I said, holding out my hand. "I'm with an ad hoc citizen's coalition called

Friends Against Beaumont, and Grady here is going to be performing in Pritchit tomorrow night for a protest against one of his buildings they're opening there."
When I'd phoned from Thunder Bay Marcia had told me about Daisy's protest, and the building they would be rallying against *may* have had some of Beaumont's money in it, who knows?"

"Well, where is he?"

"Here."

"In Homestead?" Frank loosened his fist on Bernard's collar.

"Not Homestead, no," I said. "But he's been seen driving around all over the west in his big purple limo."

"I heard that too," said one of the twins.

"We want him just as bad as you do," I said. "You're not the only ones he ripped off. Nor Bernard neither."

Frank let Bernard back down into his seat. "Damn!" he said softly.

"What is it, Frank?" said one of the twins.

"Mom said she wanted the guy who stole the money, but I figured he's long gone, and who's got the time to chase him all over hell's half acre? So I figured, well, we'll just go beat up Bernard. But we can't, now, can we? Not if it was Beaumont, and not if he's around. But it sounds like it could take forever..."

"I completely understand if you don't want to join us," I said. "Also, it looks like it might get violent."

Frank paused, then looked up. "Oh yeah?"

He sounded cool about it, but I felt a nibble on my hook. I reached into my bag and took out the handbill I'd been given at Matnagut. "This is from our protest in New Brunswick. Did you see that burning cop car?"

"I saw that!" said one of the twins.

"Me too," said the other twin, and they both started nodding. Fergie, the youngest, was grinning widely, ready to start making wedding arrangements.

"It's your decision," I said. "I just thought you might not want to miss the fun."

"Okay," said Frank. "We're in."

Farley, Fortner and Fergie continued nodding eagerly.

Then Frank looked at Bernard. "You, Reverend?" he said.

And I guess Bernard figured it must be better than getting beaten up then and there. "Yes. Absolutely!" he said.

I shook their hands and gave them detailed directions to an exact address in Pritchit which I made up on the spot. I wrote down their names and address in my notebook and said that they would receive in the mail from the FAB a certificate of deputization. They thanked me. Grady was still frozen.

"Now," I said. "We have to do some more recruiting in Edmonton tonight, so we probably should get going." And then, although I knew it was pushing my luck I said, "Which reminds me, would you have any gas you could lend us? I don't know if we have enough to make it to HQ in Edmonton. We can pay you back in Pritchett."

"I'll get that spare can out of the truck," said Fergie, and he hopped out of the vestry like a lamb in spring.

Frank was still sifting through all this new information. "What?.. Okay. Sure," he said, then turned and we all filed out and walked back around to Main Street where Fergie gave me a can of gas which I handed to Grady.

Then Frank stopped and looked right at me. "Wait a sec," he said. "How do we know you're on the level?"

And that was when Grady unfroze and chipped in. "Take Uncle Bernard with you. You know, like a hostage."

Out of Frank's line of sight Bernard shot a stare of dumb shock at Grady. "Well, I think it would be better..." Bernard said.

"What?" said Frank. "You want to go beat up Beaumont, don't you? To get your money back? And your congregation's?"

"Oh...Certainly."

"Then why wouldn't you mind coming along with us?"

"Well..."

"You'd be happy to come along with us, wouldn't you?" said Frank.

Bernard's eyes darted around. "Yes...Well... Yes. Absolutely."

"You don't sound it," said Frank.

"Sorry." he said, "I was thinking of something else."

"What?"

Bernard made a decision. "I was asking myself how any of us can let them get away with it."

"Oh?"

"I mean, who *are* these people? A bunch of rich-daddy carnival hucksters...What right do they have to come to our homes and rob us of our birthright?"

"Right on, Reverend," said one twin.

"He sounds like Mom," said the other.

"I mean, *why?*" said Bernard. "Because they know how to shuffle other peoples' money around? I mean, they shall dream of death but death shall not come to them! Their lips shall move but the words will not touch their hearts!" He looked like the photo of my grandfather preaching. There were no two sides to the question now.

Frank said, "Okay, let's go."

"I'm sorry Fergie," I said to the youngest. "It would never have worked out."

He looked sad for a second, then blushed again and mustered all his courage. "Um... okay," he said. But he was okay with it. He had talked to a girl.

He hopped into the back of the truck and sat next to one of the twins as everybody else squeezed in the front and they roared off between the last two houses on Main Street and out across the prairie, a plume of dust gushing up behind.

"See why I left?" said Grady.

"You were a big help," I said.

We watched the dust settle back onto the wide prairie.

"Ah, he'll be alright..." said Grady. "Probably. He needed some toughening up anyway." He turned to me. "Is that okay, though, you think? Leaving your brother like that?"

"'Leaving'? You hand-delivered him like a sacrificial lamb."

"But is it okay?"

"Has he ever done anything bad to you?"

"Not really."

"Then, Grady, yeah, that was pretty low."

On the way back to where we had parked we came around the corner of the truck stop and there was a police car with a cop inside looking down at his dashboard.

Grady stopped dead but I grabbed his elbow and said, "Keep moving. Go into the restaurant and have a coffee. I want to talk to him."

"But..."

"Go get your coffee, Grady. And stop looking so guilty."

He went into the restaurant and I went over and tapped on the window of the cop car. He snapped his eyes away from a screen and powered down the window.

"How you doing?" I said.

"Good," he said. "Can I help you?"

"What do I do if I want to become a police woman?"

"How old are you?"

"Eighteen. Would I get to drive around in one of these?"

"Indeed you would, little lady."

"Would people call me 'little lady'?"

"Not if you don't want. And sorry about that."

"No problem. What's that?"

"That's my onboard computer."

"What's it for?"

"What *isn't* it for? It can do anything." He patted it with pride like he'd built it himself. "Go ahead," he said. "Ask me anything."

"Well, okay. On TV I saw this cop-show where the officer phoned in a license number and they found the owner. Can you do that?"

"Try me. Give me a license number."

"Whose?"

"Doesn't matter. Just any three letters and three numbers."

"DOE 6794," which was our license plate number with a four on the end.

"Too many numbers," he said.

I knew that, but hadn't wanted to make him suspicious. "Oh yeah? Drop the four then," I said.

"So what was it again?"

I repeated the number without the four and he typed it in. We waited.

"I don't believe I know you," he said.

"I'm Bernard Jordan's niece, Dora," I said. "We're visiting from St. John's."

My full name is Theadora, though nobody ever calls me that, but just in case something bad happened, it might throw them off our scent for a bit.

"Nice to meet you, Dora. I'm Moe Mannering," he said. "How's the Reverend doing?"

"Fine," I said. "He..."

But there was a "beep!" from the computer, and "Here it is," said Moe, and looked at the screen. "The vehicle bearing the license plate number DOE 649 is a purple Limousine of unrecorded make, and... Hello? What's this?.. last reported in Matnagut, New Brunswick... Hunh!.."

I thought of that blond cop entering our number into his tablet, and having that information pop up here felt a bit creepy, like we weren't as free as we thought. But before things started to link up in Moe Mannering's head, I said, "Cool computer!"

"You bet. And you can create an alert..."

And I acted interested and let him show me his new toy, then I asked for information about who I should apply to for joining the police. He told me, I thanked him and we said goodbye.

Chuck T had not reported the limo missing yet.

I went into the café to collect Grady and when I tapped him on the shoulder he nearly jumped out of his skin and walking back to Old Man Brody's dump he kept looking over his shoulder. He emptied the gas into the tank and said, "This is not the most inconspicuous vehicle in the world, and we're going to have to do some daytime driving tomorrow if we want to make it to Pritchit. Maybe if we had some camouflage..." And he walked around the limo, blinking at it and thinking. He went over to the edge of the slough, crouched and picked up a handful of mud and walked back and slapped it on the rear door and smeared it around. "How does that look?" he said.

"Like you smeared some mud on the side of the limo."

"You're right. We need to make it more like *that*," and he pointed at where the wheel had sprayed mud up against the fender.

"Got a brush?" I said.

"What? Like a paint brush?"

"Or like a big toothbrush."

"One second." He opened the trunk, rummaged around and took out a snow scraper with a brush on the handle. "Will this do?"

"Dip it in mud," I said, "and take a stick and run it across the bristles."

He stuck it in the mud, pointed it at the limo then ran a stick down the bristles so they sprang back and splattered him.

"Other way, you idiot," I said.

"You could've told me that before."

"Wouldn'ta been as fun to watch."

He splattered the whole car, then he took some handfuls of grass and cleaned off the windows and found some rotted plastic in the dump and taped it up to one side window with some tape from the trunk. "There. No way is anybody gonna say that's a millionaire's limo now."

We ate the food I'd lifted from the free breakfast in Sault Ste. Marie and we slept and hung around until nightfall. Grady played guitar and sang and I told him which of his songs sucked the worst.

The prairie sky became pearly, then all hellfire and gold like one of Blake's prints, and then it was dark and we were ready to go.

On the highlands north-east of Edmonton Grady said, "Look at that..." and pulled over so we could get out and look at the Northern Lights. You could never quite focus on them because as soon as you thought you had, they vanished and re-appeared in some other place on that immense sky, like thoughts in the mind of God. I thought about how I could put them into a Haiku, but there was no putting them into words.

11

Showbiz Two

We parked and slept that night at a tourist information centre near Jasper and woke up with frost on the grass. I went inside to use their washroom and in the lobby on the way back I saw a box of poppies for Remembrance Day and a bowl of coins where people paid for them on the honour system. I pretended to put some coins in and took two poppies, then checked that nobody was around and took the whole bowl of coins, spilled them into my bag, and left quickly before anybody came back in. I felt bad because it was money for the veterans, but the only thing I could do now was promise myself that as soon as I had some of my own, I would repay it.

Back at the limo, I pinned one of the poppies on Grady.

"It's for the show tonight," I said.

"Thanks."

"What are you gonna do for them?"

"Not 'Soldier Home,' that's for sure."

"That's the one Marcia said they wanted."

"Well, they're not getting it."

"What's wrong with it?"

"It's propaganda, and I never shoulda wrote it." He stared out the windshield for a while. "He'd learned my songs," he said. "Young guy..." Then he paused. "He knew everything I'd ever recorded."

"Oh yeah?"

"I was playing a gig in Chester and he came to see and hung around after to meet me in the lobby. Said he'd just signed up for the army because of that goddamn song. I mean, I wrote it as a *joke* for godsakes, a *parody* of one of those patriotic gung-ho battle hymns. So of course that was the one everyone wanted to hear. And then it started getting some airplay, and Beaumont signed me, so I ...I went along with it." He clicked his tongue at himself. "I didn't know I was *recruiting*, for Christ's sakes. I just never realized..." Grady stopped talking for a long time. "He was killed the next year," he said finally. "I wrote another song about it, and...Yeah. Sorry, Thea... Chokes me up every time I think about it."

"That's okay," I said.

I'd never seen him like this, but all morning he'd been itchy and nervous, checking a set list and winding himself up for his show, looking for something emotional, I guess, to hang his performance on.

The sun was rising over the foothills with the Rockies for a backdrop as the road got steeper and a pale green river beside became a straightened-out stream in the ditch, tumbling away behind us as we climbed upstream with less and less water becoming more and more frothy until it was a dry ditch beside a bare mountain, with thin air and light that made you squint. And then we were over the height of land and a new stream started as a trickle and grew bigger in the other direction, past a burnt-over hill with fire-blackened spruce, frosted over like silverpoint.

We followed the headwaters of the Fraser down past MacBride and Prince George, where we hit a downpour that was like driving through a carwash. We couldn't see a thing so we pulled over and hoped nobody rammed us from behind, and then we drove on to Pritchit on wet roads with full puddles, and arrived at the hotel where everybody with the show and protest would be staying. The mud was mostly washed off in the rain and the limo was starting to look magenta again, so Grady took it to the underground parking to get it out of sight.

We went to the lobby to check into our suite, and before we got to the reception desk Grady stopped in front of a panel advertising the show with a list of the names of the war dead from Afghanistan. Grady took a small flask from his pocket, unscrewed the cap and sipped.

Then he caught me looking at him. "That's the first drink I've had in thirty-five years," he said.

"Sorry?"

"In Tilley's Cove, that's what Art Cheadle said. Remember?" He gestured with the flask. "But this? No. Just a little bravery for tonight. Big Show. And I haven't had a drop I swear to God, since... well, since I heard you were coming to stay with me, actually, so you must be a good influence, Thea. Doing pretty good with it, don't you think?"

"If you say so."

"Don't worry about it, Thea. Now, I'll check in and get everything up to the room. Go see your friend."

I left him and went to the door that led out to behind the hotel, but before I stepped outside I looked back and saw him standing in front of the panel, running his finger down the names, looking for one in particular, mining his emotions.

It seemed kind of cheap, and *wrong*, using some poor guy's death as emotional fuel, but if he was starting to drink again, wrong probably didn't come into it. Mainly, it was disappointing.

━┼┼━┼┼━

But outside it was a rain-washed sunny day in British Columbia, and I had a million things to talk about with Marcia, so I stopped thinking about Grady and walked out to the parking lot behind.

Closed in on two sides by the back walls of other buildings but open onto the street, it had been taken over by people who looked like the Prince Rupert High School Entertainment Committee with less acne. They'd set out a card-table with handbills, and another table with a petition to sign, and over by the bus two geeks were manning the keyboards, as others walked around with phones trying to look busy and waiting for more people to show up.

The Ratzinger bus was parked on the far side of the lot, green and sleek, and by the door stood one geek looking intently at his phone. From inside the bus somebody yelled "Howell!" and the geek stayed silent like he was avoiding answering.

"Howell? I need you!" said the voice inside, and Howell sighed and said, "What is it?" in a bratty voice.

"Come in here."

"Coming!" he said without moving, still looking at his phone.

"Well, hurry," said the voice, and Howell pulled his eyes away from his screen, looked over his shoulder guiltily, turned and climbed up the stairs into the bus.

Then I saw Marcia.

She was standing with her back to me over at one of the cafeteria tables.

"Marcia?" I said, and she turned.

But it was Daisy Ratzinger.

She was about the same size as Marcia anyway, and the fact that Marcia had begun to imitate her wardrobe and hair had thrown me off but when she turned around and looked at me I could see that she was much older, almost thirty, actually, and her face was harder, with no baby fat and not as calm-looking as the poster of her in Marcia's bedroom. She looked at me like, yes, I'm Daisy Ratzinger and I know that you know me.

"Oh hi," I said. "Sorry. I thought you were someone else."

"Nope. Just me I'm afraid," she said, then glanced at me up and down, and I felt this searchlight of attention on me. Other people around were paying attention to her, and because she was looking at me, they were paying attention to me as well.

And I had a vision of what fame must be like, where you couldn't see other people anymore because everybody was always looking at *you*. Fame is what keeps artists from taking over the world, I found myself thinking, which sounded like Blake, but I might have thought of it myself.

"Love the boots," she said. "Sort of a warrior-hellcat-princess-brat thing going on there." Then she looked me in the eye and said, "I'm Daisy," and she held out her hand.

"I know," I said, and I shook it.

"Yes. Everybody does. It's a pain in the ass sometimes." But she didn't ask for my name, and that made me think... though maybe I was just being a sourpuss because she was famous and I always said that I didn't want that, so it shouldn't matter either way. Also she'd offered her name without me asking, so she wasn't necessarily an evil bitch warped by celebrity (and why would it even flash into my mind that she was?)

"The poison of the honeybee is the artist's jealousy," I thought, which *was* Blake, and then and there I decided to just drop all that garbage, because as far as I could see, if I went down that road I'd never write a poem again.

"I'm Thea," I said. "Nobody has a clue who I am."

She smiled. "Pleased to meet you. What was it you wanted?"

"Nothing. I was looking for my friend and I thought you were her."

"Can't help, I'm afraid," and she looked behind me over my shoulder. "There's some girl over there who's trying to steal my look. Maybe that's who you want."

I turned and it really was Marcia this time. She'd just come into the parking lot, saw us and stopped dead in her tracks and stood looking right at us with her eyes wide.

"Thanks. See ya," I said and I walked over and said, "Hi Marcia."

And the first thing she said to me was, "You were *talking* to her. You were actually talking to her. I walk in, and there you were, actually *talking* to her. What did she say?"

"I thought she was you. How are you, anyway?"

"Did she say anything about me being late?"

"No. But she likes my boots. How's Prince Rupert?"

"She likes your boots? She said that?"

"Yes. And oh yeah, your mom wanted me to say to you..."

"Yes yes, she told me. And my mom talked to your mom and she said I should tell you that your mom knows where you are now, but you should call her. Now, what did you say?"

"To your mom?"

"No!" said Marcia, and she stamped her foot. "To Daisy Ratzinger."

She'd raised her voice, and everybody heard.

Marcia put her hand to her mouth, completely at a loss. Marcia does that; she over-reacts.

Anyhow, Daisy ignored it. I guess she was used to hearing her name in public. She'd grown up as the daughter of the premier of the province and was already the talk of the town when she was only my age, rebelling against her family and their politics.

"Look Marcia," I said. "Why don't you just go ask her?"

"What?"

"Say hi."

"Me? No. I don't think so. Not a good idea. No."

"For godsakes, Marcia. She won't bite."

I mean, I've just crossed the country, some of it as a refugee from justice, which is really quite exciting when you think about it, but all she wants to hear is the thirty seconds of my conversation with Daisy. And because obviously nothing else was going to happen until we got past this, I took her by the elbow and led her to Daisy.

"Hi again, Daisy," I said. "This is Marcia."

"Hello," she said to Marcia. "I'm Daisy."

"I'm Marcia Watkins," said Marcia.

And Daisy stopped, and then peered at Marcia closely. "Where do I know that name from?" she said.

"Nowhere. I mean. I know you, of course, but you don't know me. No."

But Daisy repeated. "Marcia Watkins... Where have I heard that?"

Marcia was petrified. "Because I'm late probably. My computer crapped out two days ago and the bus left early and I missed it..."

"No, that's not it. I know your name..."

"First time we've met, I'm afraid," said Marcia. "But it's nice meeting you, and sorry, I didn't mean to interrupt you, Ms Ratzinger."

Daisy turned and walked one step away, then stopped, turned back, looked right at Marcia and said something that sounded like "You're the Okum-offit girl!"

Staff and volunteers' heads popped up like gophers and looked around and said things like "the Okum Offit Girl? Here?"

And they all looked at Daisy who was looking at Marcia, so now they all looked at Marcia.

"What's going on?" she said.

Howell came forward and said, "You were the Oh-Come-Off-It Girl in the House of Commons?"

"I'm sorry. I have no idea what...." said Marcia

"The girl who yelled 'Oh-Come-Off-It' in the House of Commons. Say it."

"Say what?"

"Say 'Oh-Come-Off-It'."

"Oh-Come-Off-It?"

"Yeah. Say it like the way you said it...You know..."

"I really don't..."

Howell swiped twice on his phone and held it toward her. 'Oh-Come-Off-It' said a voice, followed by laughter.

"That wacky old zeitgeist has come a-knockin'," said Daisy. "And you, Marcia, have tapped right into it."

"Yeah, but..."

"What?"

"I never said it. I've never even been to Ottawa."

Daisy looked at her, then said to the staff around. "I'm sure she can be persuaded to give a performance later. For now, though, I would very much like to talk to her." She turned back to Marcia.

"Um... you might want me, too," I said.

Daisy looked at me. "Okay," she said. "Come along." And she led us up into the bus.

Fifteen seconds into telling them about how I heckled the House of Commons, a guy named Leland asked me to start again and began taking notes. When I finished he pointed at Marcia and asked me. "Why did you give that reporter her name?"

"First name that came to mind. I'd just phoned her."

"Why did you phone her?"

"To get a gig for Grady."

"Grady who?"

"Grady Jordan."

"Our warm-up act for tonight?"

"Yes. And Marcia said she'd phoned you."

"I did," said Marcia.

"I remember," said Leland. "And I ran a check on him and asked Daisy what she thought about him..."

"...And I said he'd be fine," said Daisy. "We used to work together."

"Okay. That clears," said Leland, relaxing. Then he thought of something else. "Wait," he said. "How do *you* know Grady Jordan?"

"He's my father."

He nodded as the pieces fell into place.

But I myself was wondering about something. "How'd you get to hear about me in the House of Commons?"

"How could we have escaped hearing, more like it," said Daisy, and she seemed a bit jealous about that. "They've been running that clip solidly for the last two days."

Leland looked at his phone. "Once every three hours for the last six days on the networks, and five times a day for the last two days running."

Daisy looked at Leland. "So. What's the plan?"

Leland stood up. "The story will probably have traction for another two days, tops, so we're going to have to work fast."

He thought a bit, sucking his lip, then looked at me. "I guess we should ask first if it's all right to keep using your quote, Thea." Even though he'd never been introduced to me, he knew my name.

"Go ahead," I said.

"Unless you'd mind taking over as the Oh-Come-Off-It Girl?"

"Yes, I'd mind. Marcia might also."

"Would you sign something to...I dunno...allow her to impersonate you?"

"No."

"You wouldn't have to actually sign anything. I can ask if you're willing to let her use it, then tape your answer for the record."

"No."

 Suppose we say it's an alias?"

"No."

"A pen name maybe?"

"No."

Leland stopped, then smiled. "Man, you're something," he said.

Yes, I thought. Something. Not nothing.

"So what do we do?" said Daisy.

Marcia looked stricken. For one moment she'd come into the spotlight, and then her best friend had turned that light off. I didn't do it to hurt her, but that light had shone on me, too, just for a moment, when I first talked to Daisy, and it scared me, to tell the truth. "I see a serpent in Canada who courts me to his love," wrote Blake, and that's exactly what it felt like, something big and difficult to resist, winding toward and around me.

"I don't mind if Marcia says it was her," I said.

Daisy and Leland looked at each other, then at Marcia who felt attention flooding back in her direction again, and even as I said it I felt that loss of power, and I was surprised how strong that loss felt. That serpent was cool and muscular as it wrapped around you. You could relax in its coils and it would prop you up until you no longer had the strength to stand on your own. Maybe that's how it worked.

I looked at Daisy, turned from me to her new starlet, one who dressed like her, too, wanted to *be* her. Easy meat, I heard her thinking. I swear to God, I heard her thinking that, a sudden voice in my head.

"This is your time, Marcia," said Daisy. "Do you mind if I call you Marcia?"

"Not at all!"

"Good. Now, Marcia. Would you be able to give a speech?"

"Could I...Me?...I'm... I mean...It...Well... okay ...I suppose... but...Wow! ...a speech?.. Me?.."

"Maybe not, then," said Daisy.

"We'll message around her," said Leland.

"She'll have to say something."

"Go with the laryngitis narrative."

"What's that?" said Marcia.

"Say you've got laryngitis."

"But if I'm supposed to have laryngitis, how do I say it?"

"Tell you what. We'll assign you an assistant."

"And we can get some good visuals, at least," said Daisy.

"Yeah. Keep the look."

"Dressing like me might seem a bit...culty, though..."

"On the other hand...some type of *uniform*..."

They rattled on. Not just lying, but building a whole strategy of lies. I thought of the red-haired guy in the House of Commons.

"Well, I'm excited!" said Daisy. "In fact, this couldn't be better. I won't have to explain why I won't be at the protest."

"You're not going to be at the protest?" said Marcia.

"I can't, I'm afraid."

"Oh..."

"But you can take my place."

"Wow..."

"So, the first thing we do is get a few photos with the Oh-Come-Off-It girl..."

They'd forgotten about me altogether.

"I'm off," I said.

"Oh. Okay," said Leland. "Now, I can't tell you not to talk about this, of course."

"No, you can't."

"But I can ask you."

Marcia was looking at me, a pleading look in her eyes. "Sure," I said.

"Thanks."

And she moved into the spotlight as I backed into the shadows.

◆–⊪⋅⊩–◆

The theatre where Grady was going to open for Daisy was a wide room of soft seats with a large plain stage. Behind the seating there was a glassed-in sound booth, but apparently it was locked and nobody had the key, so Howell claimed the twenty best seats dead centre in the hall and started to set up his soundboard. Then Leland came in and said, "We need those seats. It's going to be full." So, muttering and complaining, Howell and some volunteers unplugged and moved the soundboard up to the sound booth, which was still locked, so they had to find somebody with a key, and the event coordinator from the hotel was called in, and he said that the guy with the key hadn't come in yet, but they were phoning him right now to get him to hurry up, and Howell was cursing, and Leland was throwing his weight around, and a volunteer was sent to get the caretaker at his home, and right after he took a cab to get him an old wheezy guy showed up and spent about a year-and-a-half finding the right key from a great jumble he'd brought with him, then finally opened the door. Then Howell and some volunteers moved the soundboard and plugged in and ran wires with other volunteers who got it all wrong, all the while cursing and muttering that the room had lousy acoustics, and arguing about not hearing enough bass in the monitors, or how the mid-highs had to be pared off on the equalizer, and I thought, "Ah, the glamour of Showbiz!"

I figured that maybe Daisy would show up for the sound check, but apparently Daisy didn't do sound checks, or so said Leland, who apparently did.

Grady had to hang around though, and he spent the time backstage tuning and muttering and occasionally sipping from his flask.

I refused to think about it. If his show sucked, I could always tell everybody I was adopted.

━┼┼━┼┼━

The show was sold out, not a seat left in the house, so I had to sit in the booth with Howell beside me staring at a monitor that showed the stage, smaller than the view he would have had by tilting up his head and seeing it for real.

People filed in, found their seats and sat down, and as the house filled up it created its own excitement, like something must be about to happen if this number of people had showed up to see it. The logic is faulty, but only when you leave out the fact that we are human and sometimes behave in ways that have nothing to do with logic.

Howell was listening to something through his earphones. A light flashed on his soundboard and he pushed down on a button.

"Howell? Come down here," said Leland's voice.

"Right away," said Howell and then let go of the button. "Her majesty calls," he said, and left.

I looked at the board. Sliders and knobs and a screen with lights that peaked and dipped, not in rhythm to any sound I was hearing around me. So I looked around to see if anybody was watching and then put on Howell's earphones to hear what the board was picking up. The first thing I heard were the voices of Leland and Daisy.

Howell had been spying on them.

And now, so was I.

"This show tonight?" Daisy was saying, "Come *on* Leland. It's not my audience."

"They were angry about some funding that was diverted from the veterans. I thought you could tap into that."

"Gee. Thanks. And this protest tomorrow?"

"You go where the heat is."

"What heat? That pipeline blockade up river is getting all the attention. Why aren't we there?"

"The problem is that the natives are not all that enamoured with celebrities coming in and stealing their thunder. They said they didn't want Chuck T either, so it's not all bad news."

"We could say they *asked* me to come."

"To raise their public awareness profile. Not bad. Okay."

"And if we get any push-back we can say that it was Howell who told us."

"High time he was dumped anyway. Two birds, one stone."

"So screw this protest here. It's not big enough."

"Peaceful protests just aren't getting the media they used to. Everybody wants *conflict*. Look how they're covering Matnagut."

"Let's give them some conflict, then."

"What? Set a police car on fire?"

"Not a bad idea..."

"Well, I don't want you to be there if that happens."

"Let the Oh-Come-Off-it Girl take it. She's getting all the attention now, anyway," she said, with a bit of a pout in her voice.

There was a pause. "I like it," said Leland. "She's like you're surrogate now, anyway."

They were sending Marcia into battle, using their power to get more power by tricking someone who didn't have any. I mean 'What crawling villain wraps themself in fat of lambs'?

Then I hear the door open, and Grady's voice say, "Hello."

"Here comes trouble!" I hear Daisy say, her tone changed completely. "Big crowd tonight!"

"I noticed."

"And I just know they're going to love "Soldier Home.""

"I don't do 'Soldier Home' anymore," said Grady.

"But why not?"

"Got sick of politicians using it."

"Everything is politics."

"I've never believed that."

"It's true."

"No it's not. Everything is everything."

"What's that supposed to mean?" said Daisy, though I knew exactly what he meant, that everything is always bigger than any one thing, politics or art or love or what-ever. Everything is the set of all sets.

But if that's what Grady did mean, he didn't explain. "It doesn't matter," he said. "No way that I'm singing 'Soldier Home,' though."

"Look Grady, you know that nobody has defended freedom of speech more than me..."

"Oh boy. Here it comes..."

"Yes, here it comes. And I know that you want to do that other song of yours..."

"Minstrel Boy."

"But you just can't."

"Why not?"

"They're veterans. They'll hate you."

"You don't know that."

"Oh, don't be so dramatic," said Daisy. "I get what you're saying. You're against war. Everybody is. But suppose there's somebody in the audience who, say, lost their child in a war? What do you say to *them*? That it's pointless? I mean, they only want to hear that their children's death meant something."

"It does mean something," said Grady. "It means that when you come of age in this country, you may be asked to go off to some place you've never heard of and get your head blown off..."

"Look, Grady, we need these people on our side..."

"... And the reward for your service will be that every November eleventh some Minister from the office that sent you there will lay a wreath on some bloody ugly statue in your hometown..."

"Great, but you can't tell them that."

"Why the hell not?"

"Oh, thanks a lot, Grady! You know, I can get out there and tell them that you've fallen sick."

"How does that square with your 'everybody has a voice' stand?"

"Yeah well, until we get there, we'll just have to work as a team."

"I don't want to *get* there. I want to *be* there."

"Prairie-contrary, stubborn, selfish..."

I heard the door open and Howell say, "Yeah Daisy? You wanted something?"

"One second, Howell," said Daisy. "And Grady..?"

"Yes?"

"Go do whatever you want. *Be* the loose cannon."

"Yeah? Well, sometimes a loose cannon hits the target," said Grady.

I'd never heard him so political, but probably he was just beating his chest, working himself up into show-face, like he was doing with the memory of the kid who'd signed up, or the alcohol. "I'm going backstage," he said, then, to Howell I guess, "Make me sound good." And I heard him strum his guitar once then open the door and walk out.

There was a pause, and I heard Leland say: "Look, I didn't broker this deal with the veterans so that cowboy could blow it."

"Okay," said Daisy. "Howell?"

"What?"

And Daisy said, "What he wants to say? I don't want the audience to hear it."

"I'm on it," said Howell, and I heard him leave too.

They were going to mess with his sound.

I whipped off the earphones and left the booth and walked quickly down the side of the audience to the door beside the stage. As I dodged through it, the house-lights went down and I climbed the three stairs to backstage. Howell must have got to the sound booth because I heard his voice in the house speakers. "Ladies and Gentlemen! Could you please welcome... Grady Jordan!"

From backstage left in the dark I looked out and saw Grady come on from the other side and up to the microphone. Beyond him I could see part of the audience, and behind and above I saw Howell sitting in light of the sound booth.

There was a wave of polite applause which Grady walked into, strummed his guitar, and opened his mouth.

A wall of feedback rose and the audience went OW! and their hands flew to their ears as I saw Howell in the sound booth twisting dials, making Grady sound bad.

Grady smiled in apology to the audience, started to say "Let's try that again..." and I saw Howell turn something, and feedback wailed.

Grady stopped, glanced up at the sound booth and understood exactly what was going on. He stood away from the microphone and held up one hand to ask the audience to indulge him, then moved in toward the mic again. Just when the feedback started to rise, he took the microphone from the stand and unplugged it from its cable. The feedback stopped and I looked and saw Howell scrambling on the soundboard, then clicking on his own microphone.

"I'm sorry ladies and gentlemen," said Howell's voice over the house system, "there have been some technical difficulties. We may have to..."

But when he started to hear that, Grady ran-walked over to behind the speaker on its stand, stage right and reaching up around the back, he unplugged it, so the rest of what Howell was saying, "...have Grady Jordon perform at a later..." you only heard from the speaker on stage left. Grady walked quickly back across the stage, toward where I hid, where he unplugged that speaker too, then in silence he went back centre-stage, and Howell turned the stage lights off.

I was standing beside an electrical box on the wall and I didn't know what would happen but I had to do something, so I grabbed the lever and pulled it down. There was a loud "clunk" as everything went dark. The audience made a sound like "oh!" and almost immediately a series of smaller sounds clunked in the walls and then harsh white light floodlit everything, backstage, onstage and in the seats of the hall itself. Out-of-sight myself, I saw the sound booth where Howell was running around back and forth like in a silent comedy, so it must've been the automatic safety lights that had come on when I turned off the main. Everybody in the audience found themselves in the same full light as Grady, who looked less shiny but more real. And into the rising murmur of the crowd, with an un-amplified voice, he said "Could everyone please rise for a moment's silence."

And the audience rose in a sudden shuffle.

Grady bowed his head, the audience did the same, and I saw Howell staring out of the booth, stymied.

Some of the audience were probably thinking of war, or maybe saying a prayer for the dead, but I think Grady was thinking of the guy who'd learned all his songs because at the end of what he judged to be the time, he raised his head and started to sing.

The minstrel boy to the war has gone
With his gun and his guitar
Halfway round the world
Our flag we unfurled
To fight in a foreign war
By night he sang in the barracks
And by day he patrolled the land
Far away from his home and his family
In the South Afghanistan

It was on the road to Khandahar
Singing to forget about the war
A handmade bomb
Brought an end to that song
And the minstrel boy sung no more.
They zipped him into a body bag
They flew him home at dawn
On his funeral day
The pipes did play
The minstrel boy to the war has gone

As the last note faded there was dead silence, and then the audience exploded into applause.

They didn't know who he was or what he stood for, but something mattered to him larger than money, larger than fame, and larger than him. And it made him larger.

And whatever trick he'd used to get himself to the place he needed to create that effect, as far as I was concerned it was justified. Although it was a lie, it was the lie that told the truth. From here, word would spread like ripples from a pebble in a pond. Marks of weakness and woe would melt off our faces. Mind-forged man-acles would spring open and fall off our wrists. And all because Grady didn't suck. I was proud to be his daughter and his manager.

Then he walked off stage, with only one song sung, but that was all they needed. They were still applauding him when Daisy came out, saying, "Grady Jordan! Ladies and Gentlemen, Grady... Jordan. Can I pick 'em, or what?"

The volunteers started coming around behind the backdrop to turn off the safety lights, and others came onstage and re-plugged the sound system, so I dodged out a side door and found myself in a hall that led back to the lobby, where I snuck back into behind the seating area and listened to Daisy's show. I was sure that her songs would suck, but they weren't bad, dammit, which made everything more confusing, thanks very much.

And when she finished her set people applauded then stood up to leave and Howell piped in a tape of people cheering as his voice said "Daisy Ratzinger!" and she came out again, like the reason they were standing was that it had been an ovation for her.

So the audience applauded some more out of polite-ness, then she said, "And let's hear it for Grady Jordan!" and Grady came out, and people started applauding for real. And you could see that she didn't much like that, though she kept beaming a frozen smile and applauding along.

"And because I have been asked to join the protest upriver," she said, "Grady will be taking over my show here tomorrow night!" which she must've just thought of, because she hadn't the chance to speak with him before. But Grady hid his surprise and nodded and smiled like he was in on it. Then Daisy said "Thanks again!" and they both left amid more polite applause, and the houselights came up and the audience and I shuffled out to the aisles and drained out of the theatre.

12

Open Warfare

Afterwards there was a get-together with staff and volunteers in the Green Room, and by the time I found out where that was, everybody was already there. Daisy and Grady were standing over by a dish-pan full of ice and organic beer, both beaming big smiles, so obviously Grady didn't know that she'd tried to screw up his act. I went toward them through the small crowd.

"Thea!" said Grady. "Do you know Daisy Ratzinger?" He was tipsy.

"We've met."

"Well you'll probably be seeing more of her from now on..." Big smile, like it was a good thing. "I'm signing with her management!" And he looked at me, as happy as only the totally clueless can be. "Isn't that great?"

"So I'm fired?" I said.

"What?"

"Well, Grady, *I'm* the one who's supposed to be your manager."

"Oh... that..."

"Yes."

"Well, that was just... You were serious about that?"

"Yes, Grady, I was serious about that."

He looked around for help.

"We'd be glad to have you help *us* out," said Daisy. But before I could say anything, just naturally assuming that I would be dying to give her a hand, she turned to Grady and said, "I was just so impressed with the way you handled Howell!"

"What was his problem, anyway?" said Grady.

"Long story. And anyhow, he's no longer with us."

She'd gotten in first with her lies, but I had the truth.

"He recorded it," I said.

"What? Who?"

"Howell."

"He recorded the show?"

"No. He recorded what you were saying in the Green Room."

Daisy tilted her head and squinted, like she wasn't following, then she looked at Grady to help out.

"What do you mean, Thea?" said Grady.

Over in the corner next to some sound equipment was a microphone on a stand, hiding in plain sight. "Howell put that mic there," I said. "He was recording what you were saying *before* the show. I heard you say how you wanted Marcia to get hurt because it would help to get some media coverage."

If I didn't have the recording then she'd have a lie for that, if I did have one then it would be a different lie, but she didn't know whether I did or I didn't, so she went with the lie that covered both.

"Oh that," she said. "Leland and I have a running gag where we try to dream up the absolute worst things we can imagine. Last week I told him how nice it would be if we killed some babies on stage. Just a sick joke, you know. Didn't realize anybody was listening, though..." She looked at the mic and clucked her tongue once. "So I guess we're going to have to stop that little bit of fun. You just know if they got hold of us talking like that, well, that would get their attention, all right..." Then she turned to me, filled with phony concern. "But, my God," she said. "You must think I'm a monster."

"I have the recording," I lied.

But for some reason I couldn't pull it off. She saw something in my eyes.

"Do you really?" she said.

"Howell gave it to me."

"When?"

And now I had to tell another lie to cover for the first. "Just now. Before I got here."

She looked around, giving me the benefit of the doubt, hearing me out, and I felt myself starting to blush, a dead giveaway.

"Well you must be mistaken..." she looked at Grady. They were a team now. "Where did he give it to you?" she said.

"Out in the hall," I said.

"You must be mistaken, Thea. Leland fired Howell right after the show. He's gone."

There was an awkward pause, then she changed the subject, as though from politeness.

If I told Grady about how she had tried to sabotage his act, he wouldn't believe me now. And as long as she was winning she could pretend to be gracious. I hated her.

"Where's Marcia?" I said.

"She's gone with the bus to the protest site. She wanted to be here, of course, but she's being prepped for tomorrow." Completely helpful. Only concerned for me. So I turned and walked away, and heard her say to Grady, "It's normal. She's just acting out..."

And I thought, to hell with her. And him. He deserves her. It was a cheap trick of a dredged up memory fueled by booze that had given him the spirit to tell his lie. And it wasn't "the lie that told the truth" but just another con, like everything else he'd ever done, and would ever do. I walked away, and saw him put the bottle to his lips and take a good long swallow.

I walked out to the lobby, then up to my room, where I cleaned out all the pop and chips from the minibar, turned on the TV and watched for the first time in years.

It hadn't improved any. Still garbage, just like the food I was eating. I flipped through the channels, looking for something I could escape into, but like the television was trying to drag me back into my own crappy life, almost the first channel I clicked to was the entertainment segment of the local news again, where the same girl with way too much makeup was interviewing Chuck

T outside his bus, with his newly-shaved face and cleaned-up bald head and a Band-Aid over where his eyebrow had been.

"What's with the new look, Chuck T?" said the girl, and he said it was his way of "protesting the protest" and that it had felt weird to shave off "the most famous beard in country music," but he was doing it (I swear to God he said this) "to raise awareness." And he was gonna sing a new song about that tomorrow night at his concert where there were a few tickets still available.

Then I changed the channel to the House of Commons question period, which was just as stupid on the air as it had been live, but at least it had nothing to do with me, just a lot of stuff about a bill passing through Parliament that legalized some new pepper spray. I listened for the red-haired guy's voice and thought I heard him mixed in before the commentator cut in. Then I flipped through all the channels, then flipped through them again and then realized that I was actually finding it hard to turn it off, so I did.

I went into the other room and got into bed with a whole mountain of stuff I was trying not to think about, and just as I was finally dropping off, I heard Grady come back.

He was hard to miss. He frittered with the lock outside for a good five minutes, and just before I was about to get up and help, he figured it out and got inside where he kept up a long muttering pep-talk to himself with occasional snatches of songs and bursts of laughter at his own jokes. Drunk.

Then he remembered I was in the other room and yelled "Sorry Thea!" which woke me up just as I was dropping off again, and then I heard him open the couch and jam his finger and swear and yell sorry again, and finally climb into his bed and immediately fall asleep and start snoring like a bulldozer, then have a nightmare where he whimpered like a dog.

So I didn't get enough sleep before the light started to bleed in through the window and I got up and went through to the main room.

He lay in a painful-looking sprawl on the bed with a pillow wrapped around his hangover, breathing loudly through his mouth and moaning softly in pain.

So I yelled "I'm going out!" and I turned on the television as loud as it would go. As I opened the door to leave I heard him say "Hunh? What? Hunh?" as he jumped out of bed, bumped his shin and swore, then thrash around in the bedclothes, looking for the remote control to turn off the TV.

Good luck, I thought, because I had it in my hand, and on the way to the elevator I dropped it in the maid's cleaning-cart.

My father was a drunk who was about to sign a contract with the Antichrist, and I hoped they would both be happy. But I had things to do.

I went to the lobby and took the shuttle to the demonstration. I had to warn Marcia.

―‡++‡―

It rained almost the whole way down, but it cleared up under a double rainbow by the time I arrived at the protest which was taking place in a large meadow by the river, an open space about the size of a soccer field with a beautiful view across the water to the mountains on the other side, framed in giant cottonwoods.

And smack in the middle of the view was a billboard with a painting of the office building they were planning to build there.

I remember people complaining about it, though most just accepted it because it meant jobs, which we're all supposed to be salivating over so we can afford TV's to block out what crappy lives we all have working at jobs we hate.

The billboard was painted up with a picture of this wondrous new building that they were going to give us instead of the view, drawn up and colourized with perfect conical hedges stamped out of some hedge-drawing program, and "people" walking in and out happily, or spending family time in the many playgrounds and gardens around, because in the world they were trying to sell us, everything is shiny all the time, with everybody smiling like idiots because they're terrified about what would happen if they just stood there and screamed, which at least would be honest.

But everybody *doesn't* always smile, and the sun doesn't always shine, and everybody's parents don't always tell the truth, so why believe them or anybody else about anything?

In front of the billboard where the railway tracks crossed the road the protesters had chained a beat-up

truck around both axels and under the rails so you'd
have to climb under to cut it loose, but you couldn't
because they'd removed the wheels and the underbody
was sitting right on the rail bed. A cop was waving traffic
around it, and someone had painted across the windshield, "Honk if you hate ugly!" And every now and then
somebody honked, but it wasn't clear if it was sympathy
for the cause or impatience at being held up.

The protest itself looked a bit rinky-dink. Not a big
enough parade for Daisy to run to the head of. There
were more cops than protesters, and they looked a lot
better prepared than at Matnagut. Tod Whitely from the
local news was there, too, shorter in real life than he
looked on TV, standing beside the satellite truck with the
field of battle behind him as a backdrop, dressed in a
shirt with epaulets to make him look like a journalist
embedded in a war zone. "...So what?" he was saying
into his phone. "... You don't understand... It looks like it's
going to be open warfare.... Trust me. This is better..."

The cops were taking plastic shields and billy-sticks
out of their van, strapping on their body armour and
putting on their helmets and visors and gas masks,
becoming more and more alike, as the protesters tried
their best to look different from each other. One protester
was in bare feet, another, I swear to God, was wearing
pyjamas. But somehow they were all in uniform too.

Marcia was dressed more like Daisy than ever.

"Thea! What's happening?" she said and came over
and hugged me, which she'd never done before, so that
seemed a little phony. "We gotta get together and have a
real gab-fest like we used to, remember? Right now,

though, I'm kind of busy..." Then her phone rang and she took it out and said to me, "One second," and talked into it. She looked confident, and a whole lot healthier than in the back of the Salvation Army with blue fingernails. But now I had to tell her that she couldn't go ahead with it. "Fine. Bye," she said into her phone, then hung up. "Okay," she said, and looked at me.

"Listen," I said. "Daisy is setting you up."

"Okay, Thea," she said. "Calm down."

But I wasn't excited, so I don't know why she'd said that. "I'm serious, Marcia, I heard it."

"A rumour?"

"No. I heard her *say* it. Through Howell's soundboard."

"Howell!" said Marcia, and she snorted. "He is *so* out of it."

"Yeah, well, he recorded it."

"Probably faked a recording, knowing Howell."

"Why would he? Look..." And I started to explain what I'd heard and how I heard it... but something wasn't right. She waited patiently, letting me finish, looking right at me until I'd said what I had to say, which wasn't like Marcia either, come to think of it.

"Please, Thea," she said. "I have to get ready."

"You can't be in the protest. I've come here to tell you..."

"That Daisy is evil? That she wants to throw me in front of the troops?"

"Well, yeah..."

"It's not true. I know all about it, Thea. Daisy told me." And she looked proud about that. She was in the inner circle.

I started to say, "No. Listen..." but she interrupted.

"No, Thea, *you* listen," looking at me steadily, like I was someone who she had to tell the hard truth to for their own good, which was strange, because that's what *I'd* come for. "I think Thea, that you're just jealous."

And that stopped me for a second. "Why would I be?"

She took a deep breath. "Because Grady's signing with her?" And she kept looking at me steadily.

"That? I don't care about that..." (even though I did a bit, so I took a deep breath) "Okay, maybe I am angry. Fine. But that doesn't make what I'm saying wrong. The point is I heard her say that she wants you to maybe get hurt so they get better coverage."

"Do you know when the last person in Canada was physically harmed in a demonstration?"

"Yeah. In Matnagut."

"That wasn't a demonstration, Thea. That was a riot."

By changing the definition of the word somebody had made Marcia think there was no danger. And that wasn't a white lie at all, but black as night, for the worst of reasons.

"But it started as a demonstration," I said.

"Who told you that?"

"Nobody."

"Well then..."

"I told you, Marcia, I was there," I said, which was a bit of a lie in itself, because I'd only seen it from a distance through the rear view mirror. But it stopped her and I saw her purse her lips like she does when she's angry. Her eyes flashed, and she drew her breath back like she was sucking that flash of temper inside, and then

she patiently waited for me to finish, almost condescend-
ing. And I saw now that it wasn't only how she dressed.
She had that same placid look in her eye as Daisy.
Reason was making her cold.

Then her phone rang and she said to me "One
second..." and she picked up, said "Yeah... Okay.... okay,"
and then she hung up, looked at me and said, "Now, I
have to go chain myself to a truck," and turned away.

I had been dismissed.

The first time I ran away from home it was late afternoon
in midsummer, and I was in our living room in Haida
Gwaii, watching some stupid TV show and waiting for
supper, because it was Mom's turn to cook. Grady had
run down to the grocery store to get some vegetarian hot
dogs for supper but apparently they were all out, so he
brought home some regular hotdogs, and when Mom
saw them she threw a fit, listing the eighty-five deadly
ingredients they contain, and asking Grady whether he
wanted to kill us all. So then he got ticked off because
she sounded ungrateful to him for going shopping, and
then she got ticked off at his tone and said she won't
have them in her house, and then he said "Oh so it's *your*
house now?" and then she said "Well, it's not *ours*,
apparently..." until they were both yelling at each other.
To make a wild guess I'd say there was maybe something
else that was bothering them than hotdogs.

Anyhow, I just couldn't deal with it, so I stomped into
the kitchen and snatched the damned hotdogs off the

table (not that anybody noticed) and I walked out and slammed the screen door real hard after me, but it was at the exact moment that Mom hit one of her high notes, so neither of them even heard it.

Outside I just kept walking till I couldn't hear them anymore, which was kind of far, actually, and I came to a place I like where you can look across the inlet, and there, glistening after the rain like some advertisement for breakfast cereal, was a blackberry patch. And I thought, why not stay away forever? And I waded carefully around it, keeping those brambles away from me, picking and eating, because who needed groceries anyway?

Then I walked down to the beach with this romantic image of myself gazing out at the ocean and living off the land. I was thirteen at the time. I thought I'd build a fire and sleep beside it that night but I didn't have any matches, and the driftwood around was all wet, so I walked away from the shore, down a side road where I wouldn't meet anybody, and then across the road to Masset and up a dirt road into the woods, where I started to climb, then heard somebody honking in the distance behind me, which could have been some Yahoos but could also be some people looking for me and I didn't want to see anybody yet and probably never would. So I just kept walking up the road till it ended in a pile of gravel pushed up by a bulldozer which I climbed over onto an older road and kept climbing till I found myself in this rain-ruined gulley with steep sides.

Halfway up I heard something close by and a cat hopped down in front of me, then gave me a passing

glance like, yeah, so? and crossed and climbed up the
other wall of the gulley and over the lip into the woods
on the other side. And people say that no cat is completely black and that there's always some white somewhere, at the throat maybe or on one paw, but as far as I
could see this cat was completely black, like a hole in
space. And although logically it makes no sense, it
spooked me. So I stood there for a while thinking that
this is stupid, but also that maybe somebody was trying
to tell me something and I'd be *really* stupid not to pay
attention. So I turned around and had taken exactly one
step back down the hill when that cat jumped down
onto my *downhill* side and stopped right in front of me.

And I know it's stupid, but I found myself thinking
that if she circled me I'd be completely enclosed in her
snare, and though you're probably thinking "so what?"
you weren't there.

She climbed up the other side of the gulley, leaving
one narrow opening where she hadn't crossed her own
path, and I mean, cats have been walking the earth for as
long as us, and some of those cats are black, so we must
be crossing the paths of black cats all the time, but
though I can *think* that, well, it's like how I can't walk
under a ladder either. I know it's stupid, but I can't do it.

So I'm up the side of that gulley now, hoping to dodge
through the "opening" she'd left. And then that cat took
two hops up the hill and into the woods on that side and
so to find out if I was completely enclosed or not I clam-
bered the rest of the way out of the gulley just in time to
see the blackest of black cats dodge away between the

trees. So I walked beside where she'd run, still not wanting to cross her path, deeper into the woods.

I didn't quite know what direction I was going, and I
remembered something about moss always growing on
the north side of the tree, but in Haida Gwaii moss grows
on every side of everything, so that wasn't much of a
wilderness tip. And I thought I was walking in a straight
line but it was hard to tell, having to step around dead
branches and stumps. And it was getting darker, and
then I thought I heard a sound behind me and I turned
around, and then I thought I heard another and I turned
around again, and then I did a complete turn all the way
around the other way, but didn't see anything either side.
And then I started to panic again because I really didn't
know what direction I was pointing now at all, and was
completely lost. Me, who'd won the geography prize at
school.

But I saw something man-made through the trees,
and it was somebody's cabin, thank God, because fun's
fun, but this wasn't all that amusing any more. So I
walked toward it and said "Hallooo!" but my shout
stopped dead in the air, muffled by all those mossy trees,
leaving the woods feel more quiet than before.

There was nobody home, and I went to the front door
which was hanging open off one hinge, but I pushed
open the screen door inside and ran my hand along the
inside wall to look for a light switch, but of course this
was strictly off-the-grid, some stoner's place probably,
because where the light switch was supposed to be there
was a little shelf with a jar of matches in it, and a candle.
And I took a match out of the jar, and struck it on the

rusted lid, and it made a big warm flame which I held to the candlewick, and then watched it take and fill the cabin with soft light which almost made me feel warm by itself.

Civilization.

The light showed a cooking stove with dry wood and kindling in a neat pile beside it, and I went over to start a fire, thinking that's all you need, really, a roof against the rain and a little fire to keep away the cold and wild animals.

And food, so although I wasn't particularly hungry I took out the hot dogs and started to cook them in a gungy looking frying pan I found hanging on the wall.

I could build a big fire and stretch out on the ground and curl up in front of it and just sleep till tomorrow, then follow a stream downhill which would take me either to another stream or to another house with a road to it or to the ocean which I could walk around the coast of, because it's an island, for godsakes, so I'd eventually get back to somewhere.

Then I heard a noise in the dark corner where the light of the candle didn't reach, and I started to panic again, but I thought, calm down. And I held the candle up to see better, and there in the far corner was my black cat from the gully, and as soon as I saw her I knew she wasn't a bad luck cat at all, but a good luck cat, because she was lying there like a head of state, licking the back of one paw, completely okay with the fact that I was here in her cabin, and that I'd brought light and heat into it.

And then she lifted one arm like she was showing me something, and revealed three kittens, all different colours, and one of them almost all white, and I went "Oh!" and took a step toward them, and she made one sharp vicious hiss to say, back! and I backed off alright. "Okay," I said. "You stay there," which she was obviously going to do anyway if she wanted.

I went back to the hot dogs which were starting to sizzle, and I heard a noise behind me at the door, and I figured she must have left again to go hunting for her kittens but then I smelled something foul, and I turned and there, I swear to God, silhouetted in the door, was a bear.

He had one big paw on either side of the door-frame, and was craning his head up to the screen to try to see through.

I froze, dropped the candle, then started to back away, but there was no back door, just a window in the far wall that looked too small for me to get out of, but I inched backwards toward it anyway.

And I saw him take one paw and put it on the screen, like "what do we have here?" And the candle was guttering on the floor, and maybe wild animals can't stand fire, but this little flame didn't seem to phase this bear at all, because he took the other paw and put it next to the first, and the whole screen door pushed inside and slapped onto the cabin floor, and the wind blew out the candle, and the bear, on all fours now, half in the cabin, looked right at me, big cold eyes staring straight out unfeeling, and I smelled dead things and foulness, and I tried to scream, but I sobbed instead...

And then there was a scuffle from the far corner of the cabin and a flash of shining black, and my beautiful black cat streaked across the cabin floor to right in front of the bear's face, where she stopped and arched her back with every hair on her body standing up and her face a mask of hatred and terror, burning bright, hissing a vicious hiss that said, "I know you Bear, and you know me, and if you don't back off immediately, now, from me and my family, the last thing you ever see will be all five bramble-sharp claws of my small paw raking across first one eye, then the other, and you will be blind. So, leave. Go. Now. Bear... Go!"

And that bear, I swear to God, stopped, and... backed off, actually backed out of the cabin onto the porch, knocking his shoulders on the sides of the door, and then, outside, turning and waddling away, trying to maintain his bear dignity, almost comic now, acting as though he didn't like the taste of cat or girl anyhow.

And I broke into tears and wept and wept and wept, and that black cat settled back from his arch and skipped three steps back to her kittens who were playing with each other, completely oblivious to what had just happened.

It took me a while to get my nerve up to go to the door and look out, but I finally did, and there was nothing there, so I went back in and lit the candle again. The black cat still wouldn't let me get near her kittens or her, though I wanted to hold her, and them, just to have something warm and purring next to me, but it was like she was saying I'm not your kind, get your warmth from your own, go home.

I stepped out, looked around, and on the other side of the cabin was a road hidden from where I had reached the cabin from the woods, and it still wasn't completely dark, so I followed it down, looking over my shoulder the whole time, not very far as it turns out, to the main road, and home. And nobody had even noticed that I'd gone. And I never told anybody about it, not even Marcia, I don't know why. Sometimes I think that it never really happened, that I'd imagined it, dreamt the whole thing.

—◦|¦◦◦¦◦—

Walking back down the line of traffic from the protest I thought I could take the shuttle back to the hotel, collect my stuff and hitch-hike to our place in Prince Rupert, but near the end of the line of cars there was this dinky bar in the middle of nowhere with a few trucks parked outside, and down the traffic line was Chuck T's tour bus, on the way to his concert tonight. I figured that if he himself was around he probably wouldn't be too pleased to see me, so I moved over to the wall of the bar and walked along it until I was near the door. Then I heard a hiss as the bus door opened and before I even knew whether it was him, I ducked in the door of the bar just in case.

But then I thought that if it *was* Chuck T he'd probably come in here himself, so I went further inside the bar, to near the back exit where I could duck out if he showed up. A waitress nodded at me as I sat down behind a pillar, but nobody asked for my ID.

The front door opened, and I ducked behind a pillar, but it was just one of the guys with elaborately coiffed facial hair from the band. He came in, looked around once and left. Not Chuck T himself, though, so I relaxed, but stayed close to the back door just in case.

Even though it was the only one I'd ever been in, I just knew that it had to be the saddest bar in the world, dark and damp and smelling of smoked fish and stale beer. Somebody was playing pool by himself in the far corner, and one gargoyle in a sports coat sat with his elbows on the bar-rail, staring at the fridge in the back wall because that's where beer came from. Eight feet down from him were three other humanoid life-forms watching the news channel on a big screen TV which, sure enough, was covering the protest. You could step outside, walk two hundred yards and see it for real, but who's got the energy?

Onscreen Tod Whitely was getting all excited that this story might make him a celebrity journalist.

"Well, Ted, we're here at the Ratzinger protest, as it's been dubbed...." although Daisy wasn't even there.

And thinking how fame made everything more meaningless, I turned away and took out my notebook, feeling a haiku coming on.

According to the foreword in my book of his poems, William Blake was once arrested at the "Gordon riots," whatever they were, but he never wrote anything about it, probably because he was disgusted by the whole scene. Bertrand Russell, though, was once in a rally that was beginning to get a bit hairy and one of his lady friends told the cops that they should help out Russell because he was an "eminent philosopher" though that meant nothing to the police, so she told them that he was the brother of an earl, and the cops immediately stepped in to help. I don't know why I was thinking these thoughts, but for some reason, I thought it might lead to the haiku I was about to write.

It was hard to think at all though, with the TV distracting me, now talking about "that new bill C48 that had just passed yesterday afternoon..." and now something else was tapping on my mind, wanting to get in. But I tried to keep from being sucked back into it, staying above it all to write my poetry, because there was nothing I could do about anything anyhow.

And then Tod Whitely said, "We're talking to a group of protesters from Homestead, Alberta..." And now I *had* to look, because onscreen was my Uncle Bernard.

He'd taken off his dog collar, and on the road with the Hopstaefls he'd obviously got a lot of practice talking about the evils of Gordon Beaumont, because he sounded well-rehearsed.

"It's all lies!" he was saying. "We have been conned, and we're here to warn everybody that they can expect the same!"

The Hopstaefl's were nodding their heads behind him and Bernard's glasses flashed once, an Old Testament prophet with God speaking through him. Then he paused, and said in a different tone of voice, "But it's not like it's even their fault, in a way..." And there was another pause which Tod broke into, "Are you advocating violence, then?" to keep things moving, because valuable air-time was being used up, and God forbid that there be any time on TV for, like, *thought*.

And Bernard snapped out of it and was about to answer, but off-camera there was honking from the traffic line and I saw the Hopstaels turn and then I heard Frank yell clearly "It's him! It's Gordon Beaumont!"

And now everybody looked, and the camera started to follow what they were looking at and Tod said, "It appears that billionaire recluse Gordon Beaumont himself has arrived on the scene!" and the camera swings and I see, my God, our limo.

The picture onscreen shakes and then there's some more shouting and honking, and I hear Frank's voice yell something as the camera straightens up and I see the Hopstaefls running toward the limo as other protesters, following the action, join the mob where one protester slams his forearm down on the hood of the limo and others push up around and try the doors, which are all locked. And the crowd around the limo is hammering and rocking and Grady tries to roll back in reverse but now everybody's crowded around the back too, so Grady stops, then tries to drive forward, but it's blocked that way too now, so he honks, and that just makes them angrier, and now they're rocking the limo harder side to side. And the starts jumping up and down on the hood and another crawls onto the roof where he gets his hand under the lip of the sun roof and rips it up and off, and I see Grady's arm come out to try to get it back, and the guy grabs Grady's arm and starts pulling Grady out, and the limo's rocking harder now, and the guy is using the rhythm of the rocking to help pull, and Grady gets dragged halfway out. A cop grabs the protester's ankle and pulls him and Grady off the roof where I can't see him anymore. Then another cop sprays the guy in bare feet square in the face the guy in bare feet and he staggers away with both fists to his eyes, and runs blind into the side of a lady cop who falls down. There's a vision of staggering coughing protesters, and I hear Tod's voice say, "Back to you, Vancouver" and someone in Vancouver, says, "We'll be right back," and they cut to an advertisement about how the Government of Canada is working for our continued prosperity.

I dropped my notebook into my bag, but I still had my pencil in my hand as I slammed open the back exit door and jumped down onto the muddy ground outside, because I'm involved again now, no doubt about it.

It's so bright outside I can't see for a second, so I stop, sneeze, and then I hear, "Hello, girly (henh-henh)."

And, sure enough, Chuck T Boggs is standing there, looking almost comical with his hat over his bald head and his ears stick out.

I mean, *perfect* timing. But I won't lie, he scared me.

"Not now," I say. "I gotta go."

"You're not going anywhere," he says and he grabs my wrist.

And okay, he is a native man in denial, and, as Mom taught me in Universal Awareness class, a historically disadvantaged person who deserves more consideration for his behaviour than luckier folk like ourselves.

But there are lots of people worse off than him who treat people *better* than him, and that's something he can do something about but probably won't as long as he's getting away with how he is, which can't be good for anybody, himself included.

So I stabbed his hand with my pencil.

Real hard. Clenched it in my fist and swung it over my head and brought the point down into the flesh below his thumb, and he yells and lets go and I almost slip in the mud as I break free, then stop.

Because now I'm in a corner between the dumpster which is backed to the building and the back door of the bar, which doesn't have a handle on the outside. But there are ladder-rungs welded up the corner of the dumpster, so I clamber up onto a sheet of plywood covering all the other junk, and I hear Chuck T swear and start to climb up behind me, then slip on the mud that my boot had left on the rung, and swear again, get his footing, and keep coming.

And I'm about to hop onto the roof of the bar to get away further but then I think, why not finish it now? So I step back and sit down quickly on the sheet of plywood, waiting for his big ugly face to appear and thinking "No further, Bear."

His hand is on the top rail and I cock my knee back to my chest, telling myself not to go soft-hearted now, willing myself to go cold, hating that he was making me do that, and using that hate to prepare myself for what I had to do. Then I see his hand as his knuckles tighten around the edge of the dumpster and I wait one more second until his face appears over the edge, completely ready to hammer him with my boot in his face. I see the top of his head and then his eyes looking right at my foot cocked and I see his head snap back in fright. I hear his

foot slip again and he lurches forward hitting his forehead on the steel edge of the dumpster, snap out-of-sight,
and by the sounds of it, hit every wrung on the way
down.

I roll forward to my knees and look over the edge.
And see him lying unconscious six feet below in the mud.
So I climb down to see that he's still breathing and I go to
the back door of the bar and hammer on it with the side
of my fist, hard and long enough to get somebody to
come and take care of him. And when I hear somebody
inside come to open the door I turn and start running
back toward the protest, before it's too late to help Grady.

—+|·+·|·—

The railway where they'd chained Marcia's truck ran
past where I was behind the bar, and I followed it back to
the protest running beside the rail bed, through a grove
of spruce and out on the field of battle as everything was
wrapping up.

Protesters were scattered around, bending over,
coughing, and getting their breath back from where
they'd been pepper-sprayed. Cops were standing around
the back of their van, packing gear back in, mission
accomplished.

Two cops were dragging away the guy who'd pulled
Grady out of the limo and who looked confused and
worried now that maybe he'd gone too far.

The Hopstaefls were making their case to a cop who
had Fergie (the lamb) handcuffed, and Bernard was
sitting on the ground, holding his head in his hands.

Grady was being loaded into the back of an ambulance, and I started to run over to see if he was okay, but then I smelled something sharp. Pepper spray, which they say can't kill you, but that was hard to believe when I saw Marcia.

She was lying unconscious where she'd chained herself to the truck, one loose wrist cuffed over her head, breathing shallow quick breaths with not enough air to even call for help, gasping like a fish in the bottom of a boat.

And nobody was paying attention to her. The camera had moved on to where the lady cop had fallen, following not where there was most need, but where the story was going, away from Marcia, a mere surrogate at the second most important protest in BC.

Some people are more important than others, just like in Bertrand Russell's riot, a hierarchy everywhere.

"Help her!" I yelled to the nearest cop. "She's got asthma!"

And his head in the helmet didn't even turn toward me, but a voice from behind his gas-mask said, "She should've thought of that before." And he started to walk away.

I saw in my imagination, his uncaring eyes behind a gas mask, in a different category than me. And then I remembered something Blake had said when he was being hauled away to jail, "Soldiers are all slaves," not snide or contemptuous, but with pity for the oppressor.

And then it was like a vision. I saw the cop not as I had seen the dough-head in Matnagut or Moe Mannering in Homestead, but as a real person, with me in this awful and awesome life we all share. And like it wasn't even my idea, William Blake's voice came into my head, reciting a haiku:

What's true? What's a lie?
To do Good is YOUR concern.
Tell them a story.

So I looked at the cop turning away and just before he was out of ear shot, I yelled, "She's Daisy Ratzinger! Her father's the premier!"

And the cop stopped dead and turned back and looked at Marcia gasping on the ground and said "Shit" and flipped off his gas mask showing his real face, confused and human, and he blew a whistle and yelled "Over here!"

Another cop looked and yelled "Medic!" and directed an ambulance to back up to Marcia, and still another cop with bolt-cutters hustled over and snipped off her handcuffs, and the first cop and two others that appeared like magic put her onto a gurney and loaded her in across from Grady who was still unconscious. As the doors closed I could see somebody giving her a needle, and I turned away, because I hate seeing that.

The ambulance started up and roared away, sirens wailing and lights flashing. People stood around, bending over, holding each other. A girl started wailing like a banshee, holding a protester who was coughing and spitting and rubbing his eyes.

I went back up the line of traffic until I reached the shuttle to get to town and the hospital, keeping an eye out for Chuck T, who might be awake by now.

13

Revelations

As I walked down the hall of the hospital I could hear Grady's voice in his room arguing with a nurse. "I'm okay..." he was saying.

"We have to let the doctor see you," said the nurse. "It won't be long."

"He won't find anything wrong with me. I'm fine."

"I'm sorry sir. You'll just have to wait."

"Look nurse. I'm getting up..."

"You still have the intravenous in you."

"I mean, if I had my leg amputated I'd had time to grow a new one..." he said, then, "Oh. Hi, Thea."

"Hi."

But the nurse wasn't finished. "There was bleeding," she said.

"It stopped."

"You sprained your shoulder."

"It's better."

"There's a possibility of concussion."

"I never hit my head."

"You were unconscious."

"That's because I passed out when you put that needle in my arm. I can't stand needles."

"Still..."

"Look," said Grady, "I'm leaving. I'm taking out the needle now..." And he pulled it out of his arm and fainted. His body slumped back on the bed, completely out of it.

"He can't stand needles," I said.

"Well, he should listen."

"Not much chance of that."

"We'll have to keep him till the doctor comes."

"Sorry," said Grady, opening his eyes. "Must've passed out again for a second."

"I'm putting the needle back in," said the nurse.

"Look..."

"Shut up," said the nurse. "Or I'll make it really hurt."

She jabbed and he fainted again.

The doctor came in.

"Is he asleep?"

"Unconscious."

He looked at the clipboard. "Okay," he said. "Keep him overnight," and the doctor left.

The nurse tucked some bedding in, gave him one more glance, shook her head, and left.

I took a seat by the window and watched a fly wash its hands and face.

Grady woke up. "I got a show I have to get to," he said.

"What were you doing at the protest?" I said.

"I came to find you."

"Really?

"Yeah. Really."

"Why?"

"Because you're my daughter."

"No. Seriously."

He smiled. "Okay then. Because I need a manager."

"What about Daisy and Leland?"

"Howell played me the audio from the Green Room."

"I thought they'd sent him away."

"He stuck around to get even, I guess."

"And you couldn't tell what she was like without the tape?"

"Apparently not."

"You do need a manager."

"I guess that's what I'm saying. So. What about it?"

"I'll think about it."

Grady waited for a bit, then turned to look at me. "I really do have to get to that show," he said, sitting up.

"How you feeling?"

"Fine. It was more scary than painful." He touched the needle in his arm, pinched it, closed his eyes, pulled it out, then opened his eyes again like he was surprised that he was still conscious.

"Can you get a cab?" I said.

"Haven't been paid for last night yet."

So I gave him fifteen dollars from my poppy box theft. You could make the argument that he was a veteran now.

"You coming?" he said.

"I gotta see Marcia first. But we'll be in the audience."

"I'll leave your name at the door for two tickets. See you there."

"You bet."

I went to the waiting room to let him dress. Another ambulance arrived, I saw who it was and hid behind a drink machine as Chuck T was wheeled in on a gurney. Then followed them down the hall at a distance, waited outside the room until the orderlies came out again, and I went in.

"Hey Chuck T," I said. "How's your head?"

He saw me and said something that sounded like "Aar.. Ghiq!.."

"Don't start," I said. "I have the CSB files from the surveillance cameras behind the bar and if you make any attempt to retaliate for what your tiny mind thinks either me or Grady has done to you, I will put that video up on the internet so fast your head will spin." I didn't know what "CSB" even meant, but it sounded good and he seemed to buy it.

He stopped saying whatever he was about to say.

"That's right," I said. "I push 'send' and you'll be famous, all right. You'll also be in prison for assaulting a minor."

"Yeah but I didn't..."

"I'm fourteen years old, you jerk." Which sounded better than the truth.

"I didn't know that..."

"Shut up. You are a big fat ugly moron, and you will do as you are told because if you don't, it will hurt. And don't think that you can outsmart anybody. You can't.

You're too stupid. And don't think you can fight back, you can't. You're too weak."

He stopped with his mouth open, then his eyes looked away, and he said "Gotta call my manager."

I remembered something Grady had said about that and a thought occurred to me.

"You're not native," I said.

He looked back at me like "how did I find out...?" and I knew it was true. For the tax break... Pathetic.

I must remember to talk to Jimmy Fisher about it.

An orderly poked his head in. "Everything all right?"

"Yes," said Chuck T, looking me in the eyes.

"Yep," I said, looking right back at him until he looked away. "Everything's fine."

I felt great as I went to the front desk to ask where they'd put Marcia, and when I got to her room everything quickly became a different kind of pathetic. She started blubbering and I started blubbering and we blubbered on until we were all blubbered out. Then it was like we both decided that being angry with each other was just too difficult, and we were friends again.

And now it was getting late. Everything was wrapping up. Marcia got checked out and as she gathered her things as I went to the pharmacy off the lobby where there was a post office in the back. I wanted to send that bible back to the motel I had stolen it from, five thousand miles away and only ten days ago, though it seemed like years. The address was stamped on the flyleaf, and by the time I'd bought paper, tape and stamps it cost me twenty bucks, but after I sent it I felt like a weight had slipped off me.

Walking back through the stationary section, a haiku floated into my head, and it felt like it might be the best I'd ever write, so I took out my notebook to jot it down. But I'd broken my pencil in Chuck T.'s hand, so I took a new one off the shelf while I wondered whether this was a vision I was having. But whenever I think that, it stops the vision dead, so that's something I should think about, or *not* think about maybe...

Anyhow I walked out of the pharmacy without writing anything.

A voice behind me said, "Excuse me?"

I turned. "Yes?"

"The pencil."

I hadn't paid for it.

"Sorry," I said. "I'll get that now," and I reached into my bag.

But he said, "It's too late for that."

He was about my age, dressed in that dopey uniform that they must make you wear, and he was nervous, like he'd been left in charge on his first day at work.

"You got to be kidding," I said.

"I'm not."

"I just forgot to pay."

"That's for the courts to decide," he said.

A bit of a jerk, really, but we probably could have worked things out if there hadn't been a cop in the store with a sore hand from the riot and the kid called him over and I was ticked off about the haiku I'd forgotten, and the cop, who was maybe in some pain, over-reacted and hauled me down to the police station. I mean, I have actually shoplifted before, and this was totally different, but I kept getting angry, which didn't help. So they let me "cool my heels," not in a cell, but for two hours in a waiting room where they told me that if I kept getting angry there was in fact a real cell available.

So that's why I missed Grady's concert. I phoned Marcia, who came down and rescued me, and I paid for the stupid pencil, and then I apologized to the police and pretended like they'd scared me straight, which was a lie in itself. But they let me go, and we went down to the theatre just as the audience was applauding the final encore.

We went around backstage and saw Grady. I didn't tell him about being hauled in.

"Great concert!" I said, and I'm glad I lied about being there, because when he looked back at me his face was beaming.

Next day Grady went to talk to somebody who wanted to book him for a performance in MacBride, so we got all that organized, and then I phoned Mom for what was only a short talk because she had to get to the ferry to come meet me, although I told her it wasn't necessary.

Then Mrs. Watkins showed up in Pritchit to drive Marcia back to Prince Rupert, so it wasn't till evening that Grady and I left to go there ourselves, down the Lower Skeena with the river shining black beside us, bright ripples like the scales of a dragon, and the mountains across with bright snow on top standing out from the dark slopes.

"What are you going to do with the limo?" I said.

"I'll turn it into the police in Prince Rupert."

"And tell them what?"

"I dunno."

"How about that you owed Chuck T, so he made you drive it across the country."

"That might work."

"Well it is, like, the truth."

"I suppose."

"I mean, I know it's the last resort for you, but Jesus, Grady, I don't know when to believe you, if ever."

"Now Thea..."

"And how's your head?"

"They never hit my head."

"I mean with the hangover."

"Ah."

"Yes."

"Well, all that's over."

"Till next time?"

"No. Really."

"It's nothing to me," I said. "You can get drunk all you want, for all I care. Go crazy. Disappear for *another* three years."

"I'm sorry, Thea..."

"I mean, I get how, if you want to earn a living as a performer, people have to be at least *aware* of you. But what is this mad scramble to have your name known by more strangers than anybody else?"

"See, it wasn't like you went on that bender because, like, your plans for world peace had been dashed. Or even that you'd written a *real* song and not just some sob story to show everybody how deep and sensitive you are... No, *you* fell off the wagon because it was starting to look like you were never gonna become a *star*."

"And that's pretty pathetic, Grady. And knowing how pathetic that is, well, I guess it's a good thing to finally know how little it took to forget about us. To forget about me."

I waited for an answer.

"The minstrel boy," he said.

"What?"

"He knew all my songs."

"Yes," I said. "You told me."

He paused for a longer time, and when I looked over at him his face was perfectly still. I was about to say something, but he broke in.

"Before I met your Mom..." he started, and I suddenly knew what he was about to say.

"He was your son," I said.

He kept looking straight ahead, then breathed out completely. "Your half-brother," he said.

I didn't know what to say.

"When I left his mother," he said, "she never even told me she was pregnant. She...well, she had problems, and when he was born she gave him up to her parents to raise, and I don't know what she told them, but I guess they didn't want to have anything to do with me but he grew up and tracked me down but he didn't tell me though, when we met in Chester... My God. Such a nice ..." and he gave a sharp gasp like a stab to the heart. "Sorry Thea," he said.

"That's all right."

"And when I found out that he was...dead... Yes. Dead. Well, the ground just opened up and I kept falling. What was the point? You know?"

I knew.

"And then," he said, "when they phoned and told me that you wanted to stay with me, well, it was like...I had a reason again."

We didn't say anything for quite a while.

"Let's hear a song, Grady," I said.

"What?"

"A song. Sing me something."

"Is this like a pity thing?"

"Totally."

He gave a sad chuckle. "Okay then, as long as that's clear." He straightened up in the driver's seat. "What do you want to hear?"

"One of yours."

"Really?" And he was almost shy about it. "Well, okay...Um...here's one that's not finished. I don't know if it's any good...I mean, I've never done it in front of anybody before. So I don't know... You gotta kinda hear the waltz time behind it, you know, one two three, one two three...Bum Bum Bum, you know..."

"Sing the song, Grady."

"Right."

And it was a beautiful song. All about driving at night on the highway, the stars wheeling over his head, being grateful, and "Just wishin' that highway would roll on forever and ever." The last words he sang were "...just the highway my car and my daughter, who's driving with me."

The road rumbled under the limo and away behind us in a soft whine.

"You just put that last part in," I said.

"Maybe. But it fits."

"Thanks Grady."

"No problem, Thea. Thanks for asking."

When we got to Prince Rupert it was raining and we drove through town to the ferry terminal and parked and went inside to buy a ticket with the last of my money. I wasn't worried because Mom would be coming over to meet me, so I said goodbye to Grady and told him not to drink and have a good show in MacBride and that I would start to organize another for him in Prince Rupert when we got back from closing up the Café on Haida Gwaii.

It had stopped raining by the time I walked out onto the wet pavement to get on board, from one parent to another like a prisoner exchange at a border crossing in some garbage Hollywood movie. Halfway there I had a vision about how I was half of each of them and I was walking between the two parts of myself. But when I got on board I couldn't find Mom anywhere so I went up to the deck and looked to see if Grady had hung around to see me off.

Sure enough, there he was in the distance, standing beside the limo in the parking lot on the far side of the terminal, trying to fix the antenna broken in the riot. He still didn't have a radio, so there wasn't much point, but then I saw him whip back his hand and put his finger to his mouth, so he must've pinched it. I had to smile.

They announced our departure and the ferry closed up and shook and shuddered and I waved to Grady, but he couldn't see me, and it was too far to yell, even with my voice, so I stood on that deck as the ferry swung around till I couldn't see him anymore. Then I went through the ferry again to look for Mom but still couldn't find her, so I came out on the back deck and kept looking till the lights of the terminal swung behind a point of land and the wake started to roll into the dark behind, like Time passing, with me looking back across it.

Gas stations and glaciers and pulp mills and hotels and rock-cuts and burning fields, the last of the fall colours, and all that land, scarred and beautiful. A big country, but no bigger than that grain of sand where you can see eternity if you look at it right.

You can't put it all into words because Nature is bigger than the vocabulary we have to describe it, and when we run out of words I guess we just have to let the music sing us back to solid ground.

That's what I was thinking as I was looking off the back of the ferry on the way back to Haida Gwaii with the gulls squawking and the smell of oil and salt water. I didn't know what it all meant and I probably never would completely, but at least now it all seemed to mean something, anyway.

I took out my notebook and was just about to write a haiku with my brand new pencil when I heard "Thea?' and it was Mom, who'd made it across after all but had been lying low to avoid having to talk to Grady.

I went over to her and we hugged, and she wept, of course, and I wished she'd stop (of course) and then I stopped worrying about it and we got some hot water and made tea from tea-bags she'd brought from the Café, and we drank it as I told her about my trip. I left out lots, so you could say that it was all a bit of a lie too, or at least not the whole truth. But she'll get the full story when she reads this book.

Françoise Marie Pierrette Doliveux
Born: Reugny, Touraine, March 2nd, 1950
Died: Hudson, Quebec, June 5th, 2017
Thank you, thank you, thank you...
Merci, merci, merci...